MW01382055

TRIGGERED

Creative Responses to the Extrajudicial Killings in the Philippines

Samantha Chiu	Cyan Abad-Jugo
Amiel Deuna	Carlomar Daoana
Patricia Narvasa	Christine V. Lao
Red Nadela	Glenn Diaz
Jan Ong	Exie Abola
Katarina Rodriguez	Jamie Bautista

Edited by

Jocelyn Martin and Cyan Abad-Jugo

FOR TITA TESSIE
♡ Love & hope in 2022!
- Cyan, Micho, Megan & Colin

Chamber Shell
Publishing

Published by Chamber Shell Publishing Inc.
1007 Primeland Building, Market Street,
Madrigal Business Park, Muntinlupa, Philippines

ISBN 978-621-95553-8-8

Printed in the Philippines

Cover illustration and icon design by Danicole Cuevas

Book design by Nautilus Graphic and Visual Designs

Visit www.chambershell.com/triggered

All symbols are trademarks of their respective companies.

TABLE OF CONTENTS

7   **Playing Patintero with Cops and Drug Dealers**
by Jocelyn Martin

12   **When YA Writes YA**
by Cyan Abad-Jugo

27   **Patintero**
by Samantha Chiu
Illustration by Jewel Tan

39   **Tumbang Preso**
by Cyan Abad-Jugo
Illustration by Patmai

45   **Into the Night**
by Amiel Deuna
Illustration by Ara Villena

55   **Sestina for Street-side Sorrow**
by Carlomar Arcangel Daoana
Illustration by MA Bungay

61   **Control**
by Patricia Narvasa
Illustration by Patmai

71   **What Damage**
by Christine V. Lao
Illustration by Jewel Tan

TABLE OF CONTENTS

77 **September 28**
by Red Nadela
Illustration by Andoyman

91 **Marcos, Duterte, and the Irredeemable Political Class**
by Glenn Diaz
Image by Nicolai Maverick

99 **Baptism by Fire**
by Jan Ong
Illustration by Crisostomo D.

113 **Angel of Shadows**
by Exie Abola
Illustration by Jon Idago

123 **Self-Proclaimed Hero**
by Katarina Rodriguez
Illustration by Anonymous

131 **The Life Penalty**
by Jamie Bautista
Illustration by Arnold Arre

163 **Exchanges of Fire**

188 **A Continuing Response**

190 **Meet the Authors and Artists**

198 **Acknowledgments**

PLAYING PATINTERO[1] WITH COPS AND DRUG DEALERS

by Jocelyn Martin

"Tama na po, may test po ako bukas" (Please stop; I have a test tomorrow) were some of the last words of seventeen-year-old Kian de los Santos. On the evening of 16 August 2017, Kian, mistaken for a drug addict, was dragged into a corner and gunned-down. Caught in a CCTV, Kian's death not only provided potential evidence for all the series of other executions, but also put into doubt the credibility of the President's so-called "war on drugs" campaign since 2016.

Kian's words made an impression on me as a teacher and as a human being. Like many others, I found myself asking what a simple civilian could do, aside from already going onto the streets and signing petitions. For certain, staying silent was not an option. Silence, during these grave times, could contribute to a form of "complicit forgetting" (cf. Assman 2016), a protection of perpetrators and, consequently, an oblivion of the murdered.

But what could a literature teacher do? Around this time, I remembered Shakespeare's line, referring to his sonnet: "so long lives this and this gives life to thee". What if the interrupted lives of the Kians could be "prolonged", even just through a poem, even just on a page? Perhaps, through fiction writing, one can "lend" a life to the disappeared, like a present trace to the absent. I was reminded of fiction's role in mourning, empathy, and in the imagination of new worlds.

In particular, I wondered how my equally young sixteen-year-old

---

[1] A popular Filipino outdoor game.

freshmen thought about the extrajudicial killings or EJKs. I thus challenged my first-year students to express themselves through short-story writing if they so wished. Out of the initial twenty pieces I received, around twelve really impressed me. Touched by my students' creativity, empathy, and sense of justice, I toyed around another idea: wouldn't it be great for others to also read these works? However, I knew the conventions in academic publishing and how it is next to impossible to allow undergraduates, let alone freshmen, to publish their works.

I thus sought the help of colleague writer Cyan Abad-Jugo. Equally impressed by the potential of these stories, she agreed, to my delight, to team-up with me to see through the publication. Thus, Cyan and I started our collaboration with the following talented freshmen in 2017: Samantha Chiu, Christian Amiel Deuna, Ron Nadela, Pat Narvasa, Kat Rodriguez and Jan Ong. None of them were literature majors.

Our meeting in February of 2018 with Karina Bolasco, head of the Ateneo de Manila University Press, made a huge impact on the burgeoning project. She suggested providing writer-mentors for each student and graphic illustrations to accompany the pages of this future young adult fiction collection.

The project then benefitted from Cyan's wide web of creative writers who were motivated by, on the one hand, the idea of a literary response to the EJKs and, on the other hand, of mentoring young writers. Around the same time, this project-without-a-name caught the attention of Martin Villanueva, head of the Ateneo's "art hub", the Areté. From project "Voyager" to "EJK YA", the latter name was at last retained for Areté's "Sandbox Residency", an agreement that was signed in June 2018.

The Sandbox Residency gave our student writers several opportunities that would widen their empathy and creativity skills: an improvisation workshop, an encounter with social actors, a few salo-salos and a videography, to name a few. Fine Arts students then took inspiration from their short stories to create an exhibit in May 2019. By mid-2020, the editors agreed to publish the collection with Chamber Shell, which specialises in graphic novels. Thus, from a classroom assignment, the project developed into mentorships, workshops, and a literary collection. Because of the nature of the project, the editors and writers of the current monograph have agreed to forward all financial profit to the bereaved of the EJKs. Hence, in 2021, we officialised our collaboration with Kalookan's "EJK Orphans" Ministry.

What makes this collection particular, therefore, is the process and experience of production which we sometimes forget once we are already in possession of the hardcopy. The specificity of *Triggered: Creative Responses to the Extrajudicial Killings* lies in its content, mutual mentoring, and peer process; the various backgrounds of its writers and artists; and the socio-cultural activities it has activated.

The Ethics of Representation and Imagination

On a self-reflexive note, the editors of this collection also realise how their educational, social, or institutional affiliations may interrogate the critical reader; how their backgrounds may activate, consciously or unconsciously, different reactions of love and hate; of approbation or stereotype. However, I find the points of view of the works, rather than predictable, interestingly nuanced. While most students chose to write from the points of view of children, faithful to the initial classroom exercise, not all children protagonists, however, are portrayed as victims. On the one hand, in the stories of Sam Chiu and Amiel Deuna, one can empathise with the innocent and their devastated futures. On the other hand, Pat Narvasa de-romanticises the drug war situation in "Control", while Red Nadela interrogates the facile binary of bad and good in "September 28". Intriguingly, some works of fiction were written from the point of view of policemen. Again, the portrayals are nuanced. As shown in the stories penned by Kat Rodriguez and Jan Ong, one has to consider the complex systemic ills of poverty, violence, impunity, and trauma in a developing country.

The mentors' pieces respond to those of the mentees: Cyan Abad-Jugo's "Tumbang Preso", replying to "Patintero", captures the tragedy of death in the midst of play. Refrains of sorrow in a drug-infested street overshadow Carlomar Doanna's sestina, while Tin Lao, answering to "Control", laments a damaged future. Parallel to Nadela's story, Glenn Diaz articulates the danger of reducing the current debate to a Duterte-Marcos binary which might obfuscate the real plight of the Filipinos. In his short story, Exie Abola makes us enter into the pain and revenge of a victim/perpetrator while Jamie Bautista, in a sci-fi piece, literally puts a person into the mind of another, a compelling lesson on empathy.

Our empathy can be imperfect and based "only on the news". Like other Filipinos, we are informed about the killings mostly through the media (which, now, unfortunately, is more and more put under pressure). Kian's murder was known through cameras. Hence one may reproach us reacting based on something we have not experienced first-hand. Yet, there is such a thing as "prosthetic memory" which, via the media, allows us to "take on" other's experiences and memories like "an artificial limb" (Landsberg 20). Of course, such a process is debatable. However, although imperfect, prosthetic memory has real ethical consequences because of its ability "to produce empathy and social responsibility as well as political alliances that transcend race, class, and gender" (Landsberg 21). It is our hope that this volume goes beyond social borders in the name of solidarity.

Our intention, thus, is not to speak for the victims nor for the bereaved, but to imperfectly empathise with the latter and with the pressured. Neither do we claim appropriating the experiences of the different players in this "patintero of cops and drug dealers". Ours is an attempt in "empathic unsettlement" (La Capra 78) – that is, an empathy without fusion, respecting the singularity of the other's experience. Instead, we rely on "the sympathetic power of the imagination" (Langer xv), in hopes that other discussions continue on this matter.

However, one may ask: is it even ethical to claim narration of the (un) narratable? How does one make sense of the senseless? How can the aporia of trauma and violence be ethically expressed in a (mostly linear) narrative? Unlike some other genres, literature, and even the image, to borrow from Cathy Caruth (5), allows one to defy and claim narrativity at the same time. In the midst of the senselessness of war, this war on drugs, literature and the image offer the (im)possibility to narrate; they offer a "practice of sense-making" (Meretoja 2) – without even having to preoccupy with closure.

We are not alone in this practice of meaning-making. In 2019, Randy Ribay authored the award-nominated young adult fiction novel on the drug war, *Patron Saints of Nothing*. In an interview, Ribay, who is also a high-school teacher, tells his students about the malleability of fiction: the "great thing about a story is it gives them a safe place to think about [brutality], a safe place to process their emotions via the character that they're reading about"(Paris n.p.).

Triggered is about letting ourselves be disturbed. Disturbed, by the numerous "collateral" damages of this war; disturbed, by the powers acting as judges and executioners; disturbed by, mostly, poor children now without parents or parents now without a child. We do not want the dead to go unremembered. Like an epitaph, our volume can also, but not only, function as trace, as translation, as survival of the dead. According to Pulitzer-prize winning writer Viet Thanh Nguyen, "all wars are fought twice, the first time on the battlefield, the second time in memory" (1). If there is a war against this abstract entity called "drugs"; ours is a war against oblivion, against the forgetting of all the Kians around us.

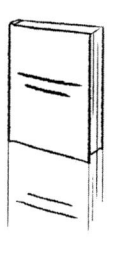

WHEN YA WRITES YA

by Cyan Abad-Jugo

've never made a claim for clear thinking. I can't think on my feet and my brain's default mode is space and white noise. Stir things up with a question like *what is happening?* and up in there it immediately becomes smoky, cloudy, muddy. Air and land pollution. Panic and chaos.

It is why I have become a writer, or continue to be, or continue to try to be. It's when I have clear moments, moments of brilliance, when I see through all the smoke and cloud and mud and know: oh! So this is what I think! And oh, so I am a thinking animal after all.

How lucky if I don't lose the scrap of paper, or the train of thought, in these moments of brilliance. More often than not, it all gets erased and there I am again, a tabula rasa.

I wonder if it's the same thing people experience in adolescence, having that murky kind of thinking, like a paper full of ink blots and white out. Or are we just a select few, those who grow up with cottony clouds for brains and who have a difficult time outgrowing this state? Surely I am not the only one still wishing on my pituitary gland to finally give me one last spurt of growth—hopefully other than the physical—to grace me with clarity in my golden age, fifty, coming soon?

It's probably why I often sympathize with the confusions of the young, and why, on the other hand, I admire some of them for their principles and convictions. It's probably why I write YA, because there's a part of me that's stuck there still working out and working through—processing—all the befuddlement of my teens. It's probably why I teach YA—and I mean the students, not the subject—I like to be around them, to witness their moments of idealism and vision, hoping I could be blessed alongside. I learn a lot from them, much more, I suspect, than they learn from me. I think it's why I haven't stopped teaching; it's because I still keep hoping.

One day some students were startled by my request: I had asked Paolo, Iñaki, and Raffy to name me some of the expressions of their generation. I wanted to get into the mindset, the voice, of a trio of millennials.

The next day Paolo gave me a list, with, I admit, some trepidation. Maybe he thought I would report him to the school authorities. He warned me there would be bad words...I laughed when I saw some, as I had heard these words before: gago, tarantado. Wow, millennials weren't so different after all. They would continue to say what my uncles had said before them, and so life goes on. They also had some new tropes: beast and ship, WTF and LOL. They had emojis beyond what we used to doodle, beyond the sad face, the smiley face, the one with the tongue sticking out.

Why did I want their words? Why did I need some millenialese? Because I wished to write a poem, and I was grasping for words, I was lost in a miasma of confusion, fear, and anger, and there were voices in this fog which I couldn't really make out. I just knew these were the voices of outraged mothers, as well as the voices of the youthful dead.

What is happening? They just surfaced up in there one day, the trio of millennials, ghosts who needed to be appeased, because they were gunned down in the street. As mother, I could imagine their mothers aching for them, but as writer, all I had was, again, dumbfounded confusion. So I attempted this poem, wove in some millenialese, all the while wondering if I was doing the right thing, reimagining their deaths, using their words, and experiencing some kind of catharsis they would never have and I would never deserve.

Kalokohan in Kalookan

Swollen-eyed Carl Angelo
hijacked a car,
his nitrate-manicured hands
clasped in metal cuffs
like a punk in prayer.
Stopped at the corner
where his friend Kulot waved
bullet-pocked arms,
so cool he sported
nylon bangles, sack pants, plastic hood.
How gangsta, man,
sige na, you're a beast,
you creek-floater,
with your thirty rat-tat-tat tattoos,
me five lang and they call it
overkill. But then Kian
has only three, paps, in the back,
behind the ear, inside the ear.
Pano na? Anyare sa earring nya?
Still he's the master gunslinger daw
maski nakasubsob sa putik
ang galing makipaglaban sa pulis.
GTG chikka at the sari-sari.
What's he doing kneeling again?
Face to the ground again?
Praying Sir Huwag Po.
Ay drag him out by the hair,
give him some air.
'Sup pare, road trip tayo
before the sun rises

shows our chill corpses
to everyone who'll be puking
about us rockstar dudes.
We're the news, the fake,
the beautiful, the good, the true.
We're the pelikula,
Si Kian, Si Kulot, at Si Karl—
KKK, man, we're the bida!
We're the dreams that went nowhere,
through a history pissing everywhere.
Ano ba, gorabels, tara na.

"Miss Current Events," a friend of mine likes to call me. She says this with irony, because I am always the last to know. But some stories do reach me, and some conversation. About a dictator thief getting a hero's burial. About children getting shot in the streets. About not getting any sort of fair trial. About getting a new law passed putting erring children in jail.

I've had my own fair share of relatives in and out of rehab, and in and out of jail. The saddest story going around in my household in the past was about how my uncle's TV went missing because my cousin had to sell it for drugs, topped by another story of how my uncle was shot by unnamed addicts robbing his house—either for more things to sell or more drugs. Did we blame my cousin for my uncle's death? Did we blame the drug addicts? Or my uncle? Should we? We know it isn't fair when one is falsely accused, but it is just as unfair when one is outrightly condemned. That's what I have been raised to know and believe.

How have other people been raised? It became more and more perplexing how some things have come to pass in our homes, in our cities, in our country, in our world. *What is happening? How can this be allowed? Who is allowing it?* I couldn't clear myself of my own share of blame. I've allowed it, added to it, by not speaking up, by letting my mind get all muddy with helplessness (*what can I do?*) and pessimism (*what else can you expect?*).

Maybe, some of our most venerated institutions have failed us: family, school, church, government, or people. Somewhere along the way, the values got bent, education got scrimped on. I couldn't stand reading and watching the news—I couldn't stand seeing smug faces and hearing inane dialogue—I couldn't hope and began to despair. But I listened to people—my own family, my own colleagues in school, my students. I realized I couldn't have been more blessed.

One day in late 2017 as I plodded around in clouds of despair, one of my colleagues, Joyce Martin, approached me. She said she had tried something out in her Introduction to Fiction class, which was to ask students to respond to the news with their own works of fiction. Only if they wanted, it was not a requirement. But some had submitted. She wanted me to read these, to see if they had literary merit, to see if they could be compiled into a book. God knows I didn't want to do more work, but I was curious enough to want to read these stories, maybe as a form of atonement for canceling my newspaper subscription, as more and more names of children, women, men appeared alongside photographs of mangled bodies and anguished faces.

And so I read, and something tugged at me, and I had no sense nor time nor patience for literary merit—whatever that was—in the face of what these students had written from their reading and from their imagining. Was it realistic or factual? I could not tell, me with my own lack of current events, but the writing was just as raw as my own attempt at a poem. What I had felt was a connection. Maybe we were all the same in the end, we could all sense the ghosts increasing in number, gathering in every street corner or dark alley. And we didn't know what to do about it, and so we grasped at words and wrote. None of us had been required to write.

Joyce and I took the stories to Karina Bolasco of Ateneo Press after that. We weren't sure what could be done. Should we have let the matter rest, then and there? Had we written the ghosts away? Was this even possible? But what else could be done?

Apparently, there were many more things that could be done. One of the most fruitful suggestions from the meeting with Karina had to do with forming a community. We didn't know that was what we were doing then, but there was this suggestion: pick six works, pair each of six students with a writer who would then give them a one-on-one workshop and write a "response" of their own. It was left to me to pick the six works, and left to Joyce to okay or override my choices. I chose quite subjectively, I went with the most compelling and creative, and it wasn't a surprise to me when I chose those stories with young characters, children and young adults. But our final list ended with a variety of characters: three who were young children (one of whom the reader sees growing up in a bizarre twist of events), a son of a powerful politician who was a university student, another son of a policeman who was a new police recruit, and a hitman who in the course of revision became a hitwoman who was also a mother.

Like all first drafts the writing was uneven, but I thought this was okay. The exercise given them had to do with imagining someone not them, and looking into the outline of a life not theirs. This was where the mentors came in, hopefully with a lot more objectivity than me, with feedback for the tightening of sentences and the consistency of images. And suddenly it wasn't just about writing anymore. Martin Villanueva signed us up with Areté's Sandbox Residency Program and opened us up to more possibilities for dialogue and collaboration.

One of the activities offered us was an extension of the one-on-one workshops our students received. In what we called our FGD Workshop, their manuscripts were read by a journalist, a playwright, and two political scientists. In the round table discussion that followed, the same questions we had begun with came up again: *what were we doing? Why were we doing this? And for whom?*

It is difficult to face these questions without turning a little defensive and protective of a project upon which we had already invested so much time (more than a year had passed since we had paired student writer and mentor writer together). The panelists were gentle with their words, but while they appreciated the move towards empathy, they were not ultimately convinced by the works' language or portrayal of characters or verisimilitude. Our students were not even creative writing majors: they were simply moved to write in a Fiction class by what they had absorbed from the news, their family, their environment, and whatever input and discussion Joyce—a trauma and memory scholar—had provided them with.

By then I must have taken the role of their mother: whatever had come out of their imagination was what was of value, they were trying to apply the elements of fiction as well as probe the depths of what they knew about the current situation in our country. So many have said the youth were our country's future, so I figured, let the future speak, with whatever language they had.

Martin Villanueva said that perhaps the question to ask was: *why is this the kind of writing that has come out of their pens?* It was a pedagogical question, but it was also a personal one, something that we all had to face up front: *why—of all subjects under the sun—choose this one?*

Our young writers took turns articulating their investment in their stories: they had not expected to be involved in something beyond the submission of a class's extra activity. Yet their empathies had been awakened by the class exercise, and these had been extended in an empathy workshop run by theatre guru Missy Maramara under our Sandbox Residency. Now they felt a continued commitment to pursue this book project.

The follow up question was: *why write? Why turn to literature? Why not some kind of dramatic performance, or dance, or visual art?* Carlomar Daona—one of our mentors—answered: unlike the other arts that could respond with immediacy to the times, literature was a slow burn. In fact it was taking longer than our projected year to come out with our book, which seemed our ultimate goal, but which also became more and more tangential to what was even more important: the process.

We were in the process of expressing our anger, grief, confusion, outrage, sympathy; we were in the process of discovering even our own thoughts and stake in the matter. Writing gave us one way of doing this, but the other side was speaking of it, and to each other. What was it that we had? We had our little community, raising our little fists and our drowned-out voices against some kind of systemic violation and violence.

Someone in the FGD Workshop pointed out: we're in the Ateneo. We're "high on the hill" and speaking from a position of privilege. We are far removed from violence and poverty, or if we ever are in association with those, we still had Ateneo to retreat to. We were in fact taking so much time just discussing these things, so safe in our ivory tower, while outside the killing continued, the bodies piled up.

But what other position did we have? From what other point could we speak? Should we then just remain silent?

Was it Tin Lao—another of our mentors—and Guelan Luarca—the playwright in our FGD—who suggested that we fight on to show the other side of that coin: if you are on a hill, you can hike down from it too, and show what you can do with the privilege given you. Fight against the stereotype of the Apathetic Atenean. Prove that there was also #Angas Ateneo.

The stereotype of the apathetic Atenean seems to have always been there. I had a sense of it as a freshman in Ateneo at the tail end of the nineteen eighties. Among the many stereotypes in campus then were the socially aware ones who wore blue jeans and white shirts, sandals and bandanas, and went on "outreach" and "immersion" trips through their organization work; always placed in opposition to those who seemed more dressed up in their collared shirts, shorts or skirts, and sneakers or ballet pumps, and belonged to what were called the "party orgs."

Maybe they didn't even have to be Atenean. As Jenkins puts it of American youth: "Youth are often seen as emblematic of the crisis in democracy—represented as apathetic about institutional politics, ill-informed about current affairs, and unwilling to register and vote" (Jenkins 8).

Henry Jenkins, in his book *By Any Media Necessary: The New Youth Activism*, suggests that this stereotype emerges from looking for youth awareness and activism in the wrong spaces—in areas of government politics and the electoral processes, rather than "new cultural mechanisms for political change," a change which can be "forged through social and political networks that come together online and in physical space to explore new possibilities." When the youth come together with shared interests and issues, and are "empowered as expressive individuals," political change also becomes possible (9).

Our own processes opened up to further activity. Carlomar Daoana took the stories to the young writers' batch mates in his Art and Design class, and the class responded with sculpture, found objects, photographs, curated at an end-of-semester exhibit. While the publication of our book seemed further away and our freshmen had become sophomores, and then juniors, our current layout manager and publisher—Jamie Bautista— decided to bring the stories to his network of illustrators from the local comics and graphic design industries.

The book no longer seems just an end goal but also a part of some kind of ever-growing and ever-expanding activity. I don't mind, especially since the killings, alongside the ill-considered attitude that this is for the good of the country, continue. It also seems to be part and parcel of what YA (Young Adult) Literature has become, in this day and age. It used to be that YA referred to the reading audience of literature in the category of YA. The age range varied from publisher to publisher and country to country, but YA mostly covered the pre-teen and teen years, and oftentimes the early twenties too. But things have shifted in major ways, not least of which is the fact that the reading audience, seen as "passive consumers," could now join communities—usually online—and become "active participants," a phenomenon Henry Jenkins has termed "participatory culture."

Although initially Jenkins studied participatory culture in fan studies, which included the transformation of fans—of YA literature, TV series and movies, video games—into activists for various causes, Jenkins has since expanded the term to include other kinds of communities. In *Participatory Culture in a Network Era*, he defines participatory culture as "one which embraces the values of diversity and democracy through every aspect of our interactions with each other—one which assumes that we are capable of making decisions, collectively and individually, and that we should have the capacity to express ourselves through a broad range of different forms and practices" (2). In a paper addressed to educators and quoted in the book, Jenkins points out participatory culture's "pedagogical potentials:"

> A participatory culture is a culture with relatively low barriers to artistic expression and civic engagement, strong support for creating and sharing one's creations, and some type of informal mentorship whereby what is known by the most experienced is passed along to novices. A participatory culture is also one in which members believe their contributions matter, and feel some degree of social connection with one another (at the least they care what other people think about what they have created). (4)

I would like to believe our contributions matter, or that they will matter, especially when our contributions merge with other books and other arts and join with other voices. Not to drown out the voices of those who have passed—not to speak for them, to stand in for them, nor replace them—but to add our own sounds and speak our own pains. One thing that can't be denied is our human connection. Their loss of life or of family is also our loss. We would like to honor and remember that. And so this book.

We either react with guilt and then defensiveness—what right have we to speak for them, to appropriate their experiences, their narrative, their lives and their voices?—or we embrace that we are all connected, we cannot turn a blind eye, we must speak regardless of who else is speaking, we have to say we are here, and we do not approve.

There are traces of disapproval in these stories written by our young adults, mostly directed towards those in positions of authority, a police chief, a violent father, a drunken mother. The children are innocent and playful, the young adults lost and confused.

There are justifications for questionable actions—at the beginning of their stories, the university student in Red Nadela's "Sept 28" wonders if he is a good boy, and the young policeman in Jan Ong's "Baptism of Fire" starts with "I am not a bad man," followed by soul searching.

There are disassociations from terrible actions. At the end of Kat Rodriguez's "Self -proclaimed Hero," the hitwoman reverts back to being a mother, walking "home to my children, my life," as if her real life could be separated from her act of slaughter. In Patricia Narvasa's "Control" the protagonist narrator even splits into a narrating "I" and a "she" who "no longer knew the difference between what she saw, and what she dreamed." It is our own world she portrays, the nightmare world that fragments and splits us all up, as Pat ends her story with: "Blood everywhere. A trampled piece of cardboard. The stamp of the times."

This stamp is also vandalized on the walls of the neighborhood in Christian Deuna's "Into The Night:" *Hindi tayo makakatakas* and *Walang mabubuhay sa atin.* This reminds us that we cannot escape the events that have taken place in our country: no matter how far-removed we are, we cannot step away from it and live fulfilling lives until we all of us value life. My heart weeps the most for the sister whose brother is taken in Deuna's story, as well as for the sister whose brother is hurt before her very eyes in Sam Chiu's "Patintero." They are children whose worlds revolve around their family and their games, but real life seems to have little regard for their attachments and their sensibilities.

I was not the original mentor for Sam Chiu, but before I sent them off to their one-on-ones, I did meet with each of them first, back when they were freshmen and we had very little clue as to how long this book project would take. I think we might also have had very little clue as to what the stories really contained, and how they were also a stamp of the times—reflecting our almost-indescribable and mixed-up thoughts and feelings, as if we had just woken up from a nightmare that then continued upon waking up. Like her mentor's response, which was withdrawn for personal reasons, I opted to look through the child mind and the idea of play, and the shock of discovering that adults seem to follow very little of the rules and so make a mess of things.

The other mentors had sent in their responses long before, in all sorts of forms, expanding the views of the collection in poetry, editorial, and speculative fiction. Reading these, I can't help but be moved all over again, still plodding on in my half-life, but realizing I am no longer alone.

We have opted to call our collection *Triggered*. It of course refers to the gun, which among other things now commonly symbolizes violence. It also quite deliberately appropriates the way that the young have colloquially used the term, which has to do with an immediate, emotional, even explosive and often negative reaction to something said or done. I'd like to think we have added our own nuance to the term, in keeping with the root word of "trigger," which is "to pull;" in the sense that although we did react rather immediately, subjectively, and emotionally, we also, in our revisions and discussions, pulled at our hair and at our minds, pooled our words and our thoughts, triggered in each other more and more responses—all, of course, needing even more thinking, more discussion, more refinement.

We couldn't be hurried. We couldn't expect to get it right at once. We had to adjust and readjust. We probably still don't have it right today, now that our once-upon-a-time freshmen have ended their senior year and are about to march in their graduation. But, as we have learned, apart and together: the process is of value, dialogue is of value, and we have to keep at it endlessly. We have to continue reminding and listening to each other. We have to never ever forget.

Works Cited

Playing Patintero with Cops and Drug Dealers

Assman, Aleida. *Formen des Vergessens*. Wallstein Verlag, 2016.

Caruth, Cathy. *Unclaimed Experience. Trauma, Narrative, and History*. Johns Hopkins University Press, 1996.

La Capra, Dominick. *Writing History, Writing Trauma*. Johns Hopkins University Press, 2001.

Landsberg, Alison. *Prosthetic Memory. The Transformation of American Remembrance in an Age of Mass Culture*. Columbia University Press, 2004.

Langer, Lawrence. *Holocaust Testimonies: The Ruins of Memory*. Yale University Press, 1991.

Meretoja, Hanna. *The Ethics of Storytelling: Narrative Hermeneutics, History, and the Possible*. Oxford University Press, 2018.

Nguyen, Viet Thanh. "Just Memory: War and the Ethics of Remembrance". *American Literary History*, 2013, pp. 1-20.

Paris, Janella. "A young Filipino-American comes of age as Duterte's drug war rages on". *Rappler*, 17 November 2019, https://www.rappler.com/life-and-style/ literature/ patron-saints-of-nothing-randy-ribay-review. Accessed 10 August 2021.

When YA Writes YA

Brough, Melissa, and Sangita Shresthova. "Fandom Meets Activism: Rethinking Civic and Political Participation." *Transformative Works and Cultures* 10: 2012. doi:10.3983/twc.2012.0303.

Jenkins, Henry. "Defining Participatory Culture." *Participatory Culture in a Network Era*. Eds. Henry Jenkins, Mizuko Ito, and danah boyd. UK: Polity Press, 2016. 1-30.

____. "Youth Voice, Media, and Political Engagement: Introducing the Core Concepts." *By Any Media Necessary: The New Youth Activism*. Eds. Henry Jenkins, Sangita Shresthova, Liana Gamber-Thompson, Neta Kligler-Vilenchik, Arely M Zimmerman, and Elisabeth Soep. New York UP, 2016.

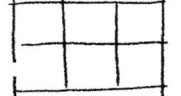

PATINTERO

TUMBANG PRESO

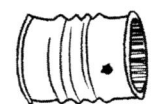

PATINTERO

by Samantha Chiu

Illustration by Jewel Tan

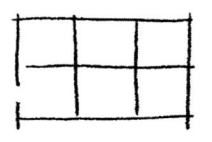

Tony watched the little girl's every move. He looked her right in the eye. She stared back with equal intent and focus. He remained crouched as if he were a cat lying low in the streets and saving up energy just before it pounced onto a rat and swallowed it whole. His eyes flickered back and forth as he tried to predict her next step. One could nearly see the wheels in his brain turning, trying to plot his next move.

He was twice the size of the little girl's body, his tall frame blocking off any possible exit for her. He had no intention of letting her through. She took one step to the right. He instantly mirrored her movement. He moved a bit slower than she did. With arms stretched wide and feet spread apart, he moved his arms up and down. He was like the chicken she saw the other day, desperately flapping its wings and trying to fly, but failing to do so. Except he wasn't cute like a chicken. The little girl smirked.

She feigned a step to the right. This time his movements were even slower. He hadn't expected her to step in the same direction. He glared at her and focused once again.

She feigned another step in the same direction. He fell for it again. He nearly tripped on his foot and was about to leave the chalk line engraved on the ground, which would have made him lose. He cursed under his breath and tried to regain his composure.

The little girl suppressed a laugh at her struggling opponent. She did not wait for him to catch his breath. She took long strides to the left. The longest strides her short legs could handle.

"Alabado!" she exclaimed, as her foot reached home base and the cheers of her teammates erupted around her. It was the code word she had to shout to claim her win.

***

Tony turned around with a bewildered look on his face. His mouth opened and closed. Like the newly-caught tuna in the wet market gasping for air, she thought and giggled. Tony! A fish! She couldn't help but laugh out loud at the thought. Tony was too preoccupied with his defeat to hear the laughter. He didn't think he would lose against Hope when he challenged her to a game of patintero this afternoon.

"Hope is our 'Queen of Patintero,' Tony. You didn't stand a chance." Mario said as he approached the still-stunned Tony. Mario was Hope's playmate and classmate at Rizal Elementary School.

"She's small but feisty, our undefeated patintero champion. You should be honored that you got to play with her," Mario continued, as he gave the losing guy a pat on the back. Mario looked over where Hope was and gave her a wink, which made her cheeks burn red. Mario didn't catch the way Hope's face turned into a tomato nor did he notice how she was always shy around him. Nevertheless, the win and Mario's praise made her day. As the sun began to set on the horizon, Hope's smile remained plastered on her face. This day has got to be the best day ever, Hope thought as she waved farewell to her playmates and headed home.

It was time for dinner.

***

Hope's mouth watered at the thought of today's ulam. At the grumbling sound her stomach made, she hastened her steps like she did every time she wished to outpace her opponent. Along the narrow alley of her neighborhood, she took steps left and right to avoid stray cats and dogs that loitered the street and the trash that was scattered all around the pavement. The music that came from tonight's karaoke session at Aling Eda's carinderia grew louder as she neared home. However, reaching home was not that easy.

Aling Anita was the first one to stop her. Hope wanted to sidestep and avoid the old lady but she knew it would be pointless. Aling Anita knew her well enough to stop her from escaping so fast.

"Hope, please tell your Tiya to pay her utangs by next week. I need the money to pay off JunJun's tuition." Hope was already used to this. Aling Anita owned the nearest sari-sari store to their home and it was often that Hope's Tiya, her deceased father's sister, would ask to have the things she wanted to purchase listed down as debt. Every time, Aling Anita would use the excuse of having to pay her son's tuition to have the utang repaid immediately, although everyone knew it was for her weekly card games.

"Opo, Aling Anita. I'll make sure to tell Tiya."

Aling Anita continued, "Thank you and be careful on your way home. There have been terrible..." As her stomach grumbled yet again, Hope no longer stayed to hear the last of Aling Anita's words.

Kuya Benjo was the next one to stop her. "Hope! Can you convince your Tiya to accept me as a boyfriend already? I really do love her. I will be a good Tiyo to you and your Kuya Gerald once we marry." He held a bottle of beer in one hand and swayed back and forth like the branches of the lone tree by the canal that Hope loved to look at. Hope looked at the poor guy who drowned his worries with alcohol and who had bloodshot eyes though no tears were there. She gave the poor guy a look of remorse and took off running home. Kuya Benjo was one of Tiya's many suitors, and like the rest, he stood no chance of winning her over. Her Tiya always said that she had enough on her plate caring for her niece and nephew, and a boyfriend or husband would just mean less room in their already pocket-sized home.

At long last, Hope was finally home. She pushed the door and the screeching sound of the brittle wood scratching against the cement floor was replaced by her Tiya's question. "Is that you, Gerald?"

"It's me po, Hope," she said just as her Tiya appeared with a candle and a plate of leftover pancit canton from lunch earlier.

"Hope, why are you so sweaty? Look at you, your clothes are so wet and dirty. Didn't I tell you to stop playing during the late afternoon? How will you clean up now that our water and electricity were cut off again? I remember telling your Kuya Gerald to pay for it last week! Speaking of, where is your brother?" Her Tiya went on and on like she usually did. Wrinkles were starting to appear on her forehead and around her eyes. She was a pretty lady who looked ten years older than she really was due to the never-ending cycle of work and worry.

The screeching of the door stopped her Tiya's rambling and they both turned towards the doorway to see Gerald, Hope's older brother, who entered with eyes downcast as he made his way into the only bedroom of the house. They heard the sound of shuffling and a thud of something that seemed to have fallen in the dark.

"Look at your brother. He just went in and headed straight to the room without a single word. As if we were just air. Air! I swear. I do not know what goes on in your brother's head. Don't be like him, Hope." Her Tiya sighed and shook her head, like she was shaking away the exhaustion and the apprehension. "Come, let's eat."

Hope was no longer as hungry as she was earlier.

As she lay on the stiff rattan mat, Hope couldn't fall asleep, though her mat was not the reason why. The mat was hers since she could remember and though there was no cushion between the cold floor and the mat she lay on, the mat brought her warmth and comfort. Her Tiya's warm embrace only added to that. Still, she couldn't fall asleep. She lay awake thinking about her parents. She could no longer remember their faces as she could barely walk when they passed away. She also thought about Mario and how her little heart would beat fast every time he looked at her. She thought about her Tiya and why she didn't want to marry any suitor when they loved her so much. She thought about her brother who had been acting suspiciously the past week. He didn't seem to hear anything when people spoke to him, and he didn't seem to eat either or do anything at all when he was home. In fact, he was like a ghost who left late at night to scare others with his bloodshot eyes and pale skin. She had heard him leave before and she was curious where he went every time. She missed the brother who taught her patintero and told her stories.

Just as she was about to get up to go to the CR, she heard movement across the room, where her brother lay. She stopped moving and watched as Gerald's shadow got up and exited through the open door. As the sound of his footsteps grew softer, her chest started to tighten and thoughts of losing him started to fill her mind. An uneasy feeling began to settle in her stomach. Without thinking, she stood up and trailed after her brother.

At first, Hope could still distinctly hear the off-key voices of the tambays at Aling Eda's place behind her. However, Gerald took so many unfamiliar turns that the voices disappeared. She could no longer remember her way back. I guess I can't go back even if I wanted to, she thought to herself. She no longer recognized the alley she was in. She knew that after walking for so long, they were very far from home. Not to mention it was incredibly dark. The dim lampposts at every corner were the only things that allowed her to see where her brother was going. Up ahead, Gerald walked as quietly as she did until, suddenly, he stopped. She hid behind a parked jeepney and peeked at her brother. He started to move his hands animatedly. When she squinted, she could see that he was talking to another man, but she was too far away to hear what he said or to see who he was talking to.

She was about to take a few more steps forward when—

Bang!

She heard a gun being fired, like the ones in Mang Ivan's movies. She was too stunned to move or make a sound as she crouched down. Another shot went off and it was very close to where she was hiding this time. Accompanied by only the pounding of her heart and the trembling of her body, she managed to sneak another peek. Her brother was no longer there.

She felt trapped. Should she look for her brother? Should she continue to hide till the sun rose? Should she run away and seek help?

Bang!

She heard someone scream for help and she recognized that it was her brother's voice. The same voice that lulled her to sleep at night. The same voice that echoed across the house when he sang while taking a shower. The same voice she knew and loved. On impulse, she ran straight towards the voice. On the way, she passed by an unmoving body slumped against the wall where her brother was at earlier. Under the dim light, she could barely recognize Kuya Benjo with a hole in his head. She shrieked and ran faster towards her brother, towards her brother screaming and the sound of leather hitting skin.

She turned a corner and there was flickering light coming from a broken lamppost but the street was almost deserted. The only people there were a police officer—from the looks of his blue uniform and the truncheon he held—and her brother who had blood dripping from his mouth. Hope recognized the old cap he wore every day and the baggy jeans that were too big for him. From what she could see, the police officer clutched a fistful of her brother's collar with his left hand and had the truncheon raised in his right.

"Take out the drugs you have or I will kill you," the police officer said with a cold menacing voice that made Hope shiver.

"N-no. There are no drugs. Kuya Benjo—"

The police officer hit him on the side of his head with the truncheon.

Her brother winced in pain and coughed blood out.

"Tell the truth, kid," the police officer said as he raised the truncheon in the air for the second time.

"P-please let m-me go home. M-my Tiya. M-my sister… N-no drugs…" Gerald said as he quivered under the hold of the police officer. The same feeling in her chest tightened further. Hope couldn't understand what was going on, but all she knew was that her brother was in danger and she didn't want to lose him.

Hope rushed forward, intending to save her brother. The police officer turned around.

Her heart raced faster.

The silence returned.

Her hands shook.

He watched the little girl's every move. She eyed him warily as she took sidesteps from left to right. His eyes flickered back and forth with amusement as he tried to predict her next move. She looked him right in the eye. He stared back with equal intent and focus.

He was thrice the size of the little girl's body, his tall frame blocking off any possible exit for her. He had no intention of letting her through. She took one step to the right. He mirrored her movement as quickly as he could. He won't be able to stop me, she thought. The little girl smirked.

She feigned a step to the right. This time his movement was a lot more sluggish as she expected. However, shock seemed to register on his face at being fooled and being outpaced. He glared at her and focused once again.

She feigned another step in the same direction. He fell for it again. He nearly tripped on his foot. She heard him curse under his breath and saw him try to regain his composure.

The little girl suppressed a laugh at her struggling opponent. Not waiting for him to catch his breath, she took the longest strides her short legs could handle to the left.

"Kuya!" She exclaimed as she reached for her brother, who was watching with horror. She wrapped her arms around her brother as best as she could. She had defeated the police officer. A look of triumph slowly flooded her face.

Bang!

Hope felt something bury itself into her skin. Pain. Pain was the only thing that registered in her mind. But as her body hit the pavement, she could no longer feel anything. Numbness came. Before blacking out, one last thought came to her mind. She was caught. It was the first time she had lost a game of patintero.

"My story basically started with the concept. I thought of the idea that the people in power just see this all as a game, because they're all up there. They're not with the people who are dying, the innocent people getting killed. For me, it started there. I wanted my story to revolve around that concept wherein it's just a game. And that's where patintero comes into play. Patintero is a game wherein you have people tagging or trying to catch someone and there are people who are trying to escape. I was thinking it was quite similar to what was happening now. There are people who are innocent just trying to pass by and escape this whole fiasco that shouldn't be happening in their everyday life. They're just ordinary people who are getting involved and there are policemen who are catching them. Afterwards, I started to think of the persona that I wanted to use for the story. I thought that I can't possibly assume or know what it's like to be the main victim or what it's like to be in the perpetrator's perspective. Therefore, I decided to go with someone more innocent: a child. I used the perspective of a child who really had nothing to do with this. The kid in my story is very young. I mean, what could she possibly know about EJK or drugs or the people who started all this? Overall, it was really about how people in power look at the game and how a child looks at the game. It just flowed from there."

Samantha Chiu
on writing her story "Patintero"

TUMBANG PRESO

by Cyan Abad-Jugo

Illustration by Patmai

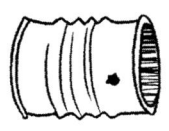

Kuya, sige na,
please play with us,
stay in the circle, and
with your long arms
and longer strides
whirl us around our squealing.
Now we can barely take aim at the can
that we must topple with our slippers
the Carnation Evap on the asphalt
within striking distance.

Manong, ano ba,
please stay away,
why scuff the circle, and
with your men at arms
and beating sticks
press upon Kuya screaming.
Now we cannot see who aims the kick
that topples him on orphan slippers
red carnage on the asphalt
withholding our future.

Kayo po, tayo na,
please pray with us,
form the circle, and
with your raised arms
and beating hearts
remember Kuya with our sighing.
Now we aim this grief
to topple our sightless prisons
restoring dented can on asphalt
withstanding death.

INTO THE NIGHT

SESTINA FOR STREET-SIDE SORROW

INTO THE NIGHT

by Amiel Deuna

Illustration by Ara Villena

The downpour finally stopped as Melody gazed through the small window of their family's bedroom at the gloomy evening clouds. Water dripped from the edges of their house's roof, so she tried to reach out to the small globes of water. To her dismay, she couldn't reach the droplets as they were just a few inches short of her fingertips. She slowly turned her head to glance at the muddy ground. The droplets formed a small puddle that showed her reflection. Seeing her milky-white face and her long, black hair, the figure turned distorted as the droplets rippled the puddle. She laughed as she watched the rippling of the water. The wavelets slowed to a stop and she quickly lifted her head to gaze at the gleaming stars of the sky. They shone bright, and staring at the light, she wondered if she could reach it.

"Mel, tumigil na 'yung ulan. Punta na tayo kay Aling Nena," Alfred yelled, disrupting the silence.

Melody rushed to the entrance of the house. Alfred met her outside the door, along the street. It was time to for their nightly visit to the sari-sari store five minutes away from their house.

"Kinalimutan mo na 'yung blanket mo, o. Ako na maglalagay sa iyo," he said with a comforting voice. The blanket protected her from the cold fog that could make her sick. Mel ducked and tried to escape from Alfred's embrace.

"Mel, isuot mo na 'to. Baka magkasakit ka pa. Malapit na 'yung exam mo," he insisted.

"Sige na nga. Pero, once I'm ten, wala na ha."

"Naku, kahit hanggang 20 ka na, lalagyan pa rin kita ng blanket," Alfred said, which made both of them laugh.

The sari-sari store was right around the corner, making it convenient for a lot of the residents nearby. The store was along a street that was always bustling; there were always people and cars passing through that block, where houses leaned on one side of the street and a huge wall ran alongside the other, with graffiti like "HINDI TAYO MAKAKATAKAS" and "WALANG MABUBUHAY SA ATIN" painted across it. The houses all had the same design: unpainted cement walls, rusted roofs, wooden doors, small windows, and slippers lined up in front of the houses. They walked in silence, both holding each other's hands, until they arrived at the sari-sari store.

Aling Nena's sari-sari store was pretty popular among the people in their neighborhood. Usually at around that time, a lot of people—from small kids who wanted to buy candy to middle-aged men buying beer while gambling—would stop by and just stay there until it would get late at night. Two small tables were set up in front of the store, and one of the tables was occupied by a few men who were drinking beer while listening to the radio. The other table, however, was used by three women gossiping. Their voices were so loud that Melody could hear almost every insult they muttered.

"Wala nang ginagawa yung mga iyan. Hindi na sila kumikita."

"Kawawa naman yung mga pamilya nila. Pang-inom na lang yung iniipon na pera ng kanilang mga asawa."

"Tingnan mo, o. Bagsak na naman si Romel. Mababatukan na naman 'yan ng kaniyang nanay."

As the two siblings passed by the tables, Mel saw the glaring eyes of the women.

The sari-sari store was simple; it was a small counter with metal bars separating them from Aling Nena. She was wearing her usual outfit: a light blue apron on top of her white shirt. She was rummaging for something in the counter when Alfred called her.

"Aling Nena, pabili po ng Coke at empanada," Alfred said. These were the usual things that they would order at the sari-sari store. Upon hearing Alfred's voice, she looked up and smiled.

While Alfred conversed with Aling Nena, Melody overheard what was being broadcasted over the radio.

"Babala sa mga taga-Tondo: ngayong gabi, maaaring magkaroon ng raid sa mga kalsada sa Tondo upang hanapin ang mga drug pushers sa Manila," the newscaster reported. This caused a sudden commotion by the people on the tables. The drunk men began ranting about the current government, while the women speculated about the possible raid.

"Hala, may raid daw ngayon. 'Di ba dapat na tayong umalis?" One woman asked the other ladies.

"'Wag kang mag-alala. 'Yung mga drug users lang naman ang lalagutin nila," another woman responded.

"Oo nga," the third woman said. "Diba wala naman tayong ginagawang masama? Safe tayo. Pero…" she stopped and glanced at Alfred.

She noticed that Melody was staring at her, and that made the woman look in the opposite direction. Mel, feeling uneasy, suddenly grabbed her brother's hand, and Alfred responded by squeezing hers lightly.

"Okay lang tayo, Mel." Alfred said in a firm voice. "'Wag mo silang alalahanin"

Somehow, the presence of her brother made her feel safe. She felt like it was all that she needed. Alfred, after offering her the empanada and the clear, small plastic bag filled with Coke, wrapped the blanket around her again. It was starting to get late.

On the trip back home, they walked side by side, eating their empanadas and slurping at their drinks. They were so focused on eating that they found themselves at home already. It was the same as every other house in their street, except for the fact that someone was lying down in front of theirs. Marcela, their mother, passed out on the street. It was a habit of hers to leave them in the afternoon and come back home drunk, although this was the first time she actually slept in front of their house. Alfred carried her motionless body inside the house and laid her down on the sofa. She was stirring, and they could hear her mutter the name "Joel" repeatedly.

Joel was the name of their mother's first husband. He was the father of Alfred, while Melody was the daughter of Marcela's second man. Marcela's relationship with Joel didn't end well, and it caused her to despise Alfred so much.

Marcela was still sleeping heavily so they started cleaning up around her. Although silence filled the air, they were perfectly synchronized as they continued their nightly chores. They both washed the dishes as if they were one person: Alfred sponged the plates while Mel wiped them dry. Alfred playfully splashed a bit of water on Mel, and she retaliated by slapping him with the dish towel.

Their house wasn't something to brag about. It had two rooms: one for sleeping and the other for everything else. The living area had a small couch with an old plasma television across it, and beside it was the kitchen with a dining table that would fit four people. After a change of clothes, Melody proceeded to the bedroom. The bedroom was small compared to the living room, but it was sufficient for the three of them. A sleeping mat was already set on the floor, and three pillows were placed beside each other. Melody would always get the largest one, and she would always sleep between Alfred and their mother.

Instead of lying down immediately to rest, she looked out their one window and up at the stars. She stared with awe at the gleaming balls of light, and her eyes got lost at the wonders of the sky. She was feeling tired from what happened already, and she almost fell asleep beside the windowpane. Thankfully, Alfred was there to lead her to the sleeping mat.

She woke up a few hours after, and heard footsteps marching into their house. Melody felt her brother sit up beside her.

"Saan po ma'am?" Melody heard.

"Diyan sa loob. 'Yung lalaki," her mother's voice replied. "Kunin mo na siya."

They heard swift steps coming closer towards the bedroom and then the door flew open. A dozen policemen crowded the entryway, and most of them were holding guns. They glared at Alfred, and on impulse, Melody wrapped her arms around her brother. She held him as tight as possible while the policemen tried to pry her away from him. Mel felt a blow on her back and this caused her to lose her grip on her brother. Alfred instantly reached for Melody, but was immediately pinned down by three policemen. He started to kick and push away at them, but stopped when their mother screamed out loud.

"Siya! Siya yung pusher!" It was obvious that she was still under the influence of alcohol, despite her endless sleep a while ago.

"Hindi ako! Wala akong ginagawa. Hindi talaga ako!" Alfred shouted as the policemen dragged him to his feet.

Melody tried to run after them, but a policeman kept her there and the door was shut so that she could not get out. The policeman from the other side of the door was too strong for her, so she couldn't do anything but listen to what was happening at the other side. She shivered, her hands shook, tears fell from her eyes. She clenched her hands, listening to punches, screams, and then—two gunshots.

The whole house was suddenly silent, though she could still hear the echo of the shots. She reached for her blanket and wrapped it around her, the deafening silence resonating throughout the room. It took all her strength to open the plywood door.

Melody stared at the cluttered chaos around her. She could not figure out if it was her house or not. All of the furniture toppled over, everything broken, nothing was recognizable. There were streaks of red on the unpainted wall. Below it, the motionless body of her mother lay on the floor with her eyes looking towards the open doorway. The bullet wound was on her forehead, a gaping hole straight clean.

Melody screamed. She sat down beside her mother, hugging the lifeless body, soaking her clothes, as well as the blanket, in blood. She was about to lie down beside her mother when she realized Alfred was missing. There had been two gunshots. There was only one wound on Marcela. Melody staggered up and ran straight out of the house.

She could see the chaos happening in the street—a few dead bodies lying on the ground, their neighbors crying over loved ones, bystanders watching the commotion, policemen writing reports on the drug raid, and ambulance care assistants tending to those who got hurt during the raid. There was a lot of shouting, crying, and pushing everywhere.

Melody pressed past all of them. It was tough for her; everyone was more than a foot taller, so it was hard for her to see where she was going. Random people started shoving her, stepping on her bare feet. Her blanket was missing, but there was no time to go back for it. She needed to look for her brother. Alfred meant everything to her, and nothing else mattered.

Melody pushed back at the crowd with all of her might, elbowing her way past the men, women and children scrambling along the street. There was no time to lose. She quickened her pace, leaving the clamor behind. She swiftly passed the sari-sari store while the people at the tables called to her. Nothing else mattered but Alfred.

She didn't stop. She ran on and on, into the night.

"When I was given this assignment I really wanted to base it off of an actual event or recent event that happened. So I remembered there was a police operation in Tondo, Manila around August 2017. It was one of their large operations because a lot of people were arrested and around twenty people were killed. I drew inspiration from that. I was thinking about how a lot of the news was focused on the people who were killed and arrested, whereas in reality they are not the only people who were affected. For my story, I focused on the dynamics of the family. I was thinking, 'Oh, why aren't they also focusing on the family members who were affected by this?' I really wanted to highlight that and show that it's not just the killers or the people who were arrested that were affected, but also their family members who are grieving and mourning and trying to struggle to find themselves especially after everything that happened during that event."

Amiel Deuna
on writing his story "Into the Night"

SESTINA FOR STREET-SIDE SORROW

by Carlomar Arcangel Daoana

Illustration by MA Bungay

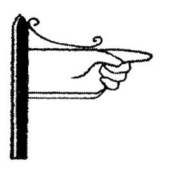

Nothing famous ever came out of Cuatro de Julio,
The street that always interrupted the sleep
Of its inhabitants, including my grandmother's,
Who had to listen through the bawling sorrow
Of drunkards, the scampering of the police,
All of us under their mercy: our inheritance.

Largely debt and unhappiness, our inheritance
Was not visible to those living outside Cuatro de Julio—
If it were, other people, especially the police,
Would have been more forgiving, allowing our sleep,
Our silence and our poverty. Exposed to sorrow
Like salt, we swallowed our tears, like grandmother.

Setting up a house by the street, my grandmother
Soldiered through a husbandless life, her inheritance
From God. No one was a witness to this sorrow
Except her five children and Cuatro de Julio
Which, in its early years, was conducive for sleep.
They would be meddlesome decades later, the police.

Once, on my way to public school, I saw the police
Chase my cousins for drug pushing. My grandmother
Never intervened. Soap operas and afternoon sleep
Were her chosen companions, her inheritance.
For living so long in a street called Cuatro de Julio
She should have been spared from this kind of sorrow.

Sometimes, like shabu or cough syrup, sorrow
Could be addictive. Even the steadfast among the police
Are honeycombed by it. Patrolling Cuatro de Julio,
What wild sadness were they storing? My grandmother
Could teach them a thing about this native inheritance
So instead of beating their wives, they could sleep.

In a riot or in the stoning of our house, I feigned sleep.
There's a limit to a boy's body in containing sorrow;
Feverish, I once wept complainingly over this inheritance.
They were busy searching another's house, the police
But I knew she heard me loud and clear, my grandmother.
In shame, I would write my address as Fourth of July.

Grandmother, forgive me for forsaking my inheritance.
I may have left Cuatro de Julio but not its sorrow.
The police have one less thing to worry about now. Sleep.

CONTROL

WHAT DAMAGE

CONTROL

by Patricia Narvasa

Illustration by Patmai

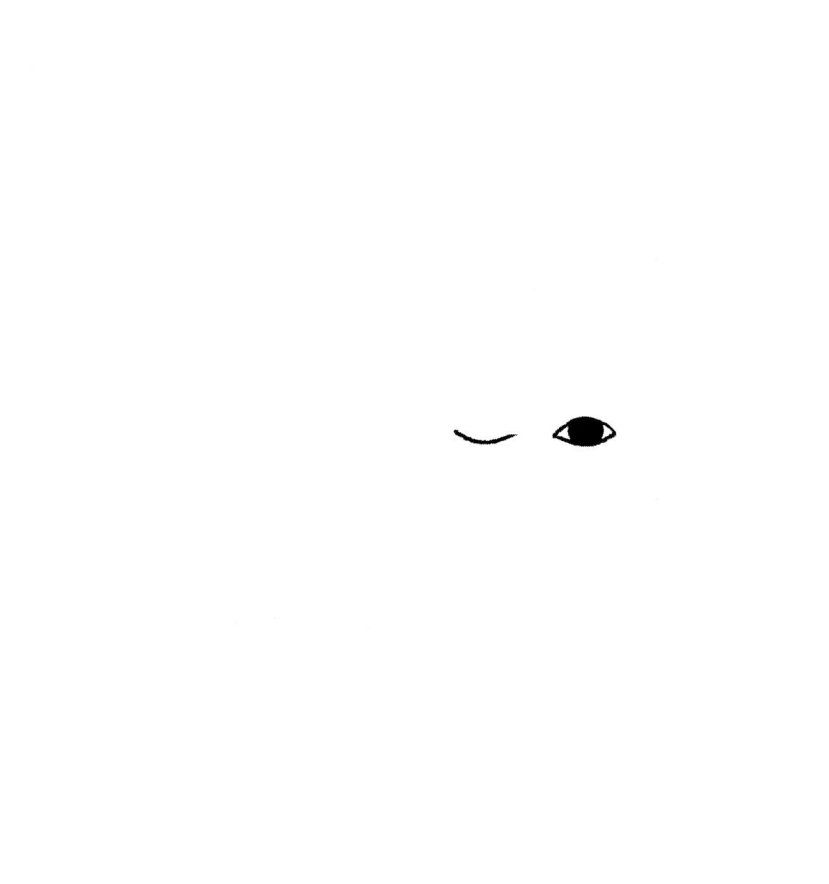

I remember that week like it was yesterday. I was five years old and I was starting to understand people and their actions. I was five and eager to learn about the world, but instead that curiosity was replaced by fear. Not by monsters hiding under my bed or villains from fairy tales, but from the reality I lived in. At five years old, I learned the world I lived in was one filled with many horrors, monsters that are created by people.

Fear. It's not something that I could just forget. It was the way my parents exchanged glances. The way Papa cursed under his breath. The watery eyes of Mama. The fake smiles they always wore. They were so afraid that something was going to happen. They were always looking over their shoulders and telling me to always stay close to them. They were being overly cautious. Eventually, I too learned that you could never be too careful, if you have something to be afraid of.

I overheard Lolo and Lola talking about something Papa did, but I didn't understand what was happening. All I knew was that something was very wrong. Then that fateful day. I was playing with my dolls when all of a sudden, men came in, and then bang, bang, bang.

Just like falling asleep, everything faded to black.

It felt like falling asleep but I know I died that day. I died and nothing was ever the same again.

I know I died but I woke up the next day. I should have been in heaven with Papa Jesus and Mama Mary, but instead I woke up, and it felt like hell. It still does. I woke up no longer in control of my body. Instead I woke up watching myself, hearing my thoughts, feeling my emotions. It was all me, but I was no longer in control. My thoughts, my actions and my feelings were no longer mine. I was no longer myself. Yet, I was stuck with her, watching her live the life that I should have lived.

I used to be the center of my family's world. I was the only child and the only grandchild. Papa would always buy me dolls. Everyday Papa would go to work and Mama would stay home and play with me, but Papa would always be home right before dinner. We were always complete for dinner—Lolo, Lola, Mama, Papa and me. Dinner time was filled with me talking. I would always ask questions about their day, what Papa did at work, how Papa and Mama met, why Mama didn't have a job like Papa, why Lolo only had hair on the back of his head, why Lola always cooked the best food and a million more questions. Then of course, I would tell them everything I did that day. I'd tell them what my dolls and I played that afternoon, or I'd show them the new family picture that I drew that day. It was what we always did.

Now Mama still stays at home with her, and they still have dinner together—Lolo, Lola, Mama and her. But there is no Papa for her to ask what he did at work, and there is no one who gives her toys. They don't even realize that the body there sitting with them, talking with them, isn't me. No one misses me.

They sent her to school just as they had planned to send me. She did really well, the one with her hand always raised, her quizzes perfect or near perfect, and she easily made friends with everyone. She was always excited to learn, looked at the world with curiosity and excelled in everything she tried, every sport and art. That was my life she was living. Her promise—to become someone remarkable, someone powerful and exceptional—was supposed to be mine.

One night during dinner, she asked Mama where Papa went. Mama looked panicked, unsure of what to say. Mama asked her about school.

Then, the following day, in one of her classes, the teacher talked about how horrible drug users were, how they were the source of everyone's problems. She had her hand raised, ready to share some idea, when she met her teacher's eyes. Those eyes looked back at her with disgust, and at that moment, something changed for her.

Those eyes, they belonged to someone else, but whose? At that moment, she was no longer staring at her teacher, but at a man she didn't know. A man with dark brown eyes, an almost-balding head. He towered over her. She didn't know him, neither did I. But why did he seem so familiar?

"What is your answer?"

She started.

Her teacher said, impatiently, "Stop daydreaming."

She felt heat rush up to her face as all her classmates erupted in laughter.

Days later, all she could think about was that man she saw. Why couldn't she remember where he was from? Why can't I?

Afterwards, the dreams began to take over her days. In the middle of class, the world would slowly dim. A series of images would swirl around her. Papa. Dolls. Disturbing sounds. Shouts. Incoherent shouts. Cries. Screams.

The man. A gun.

Bang.

Bang.

Bang.

Darkness.

Confused, frightened, and distracted in class, she withdrew from discussions, from her teachers and friends. Soon, they whispered about her strangeness. But all she could hear were the sounds coming from another world. She no longer knew the difference between what she saw, and what she dreamed.

Mama should know, right? Mama could explain to her what I already knew: this was about Papa. If we knew where Papa was, maybe the visions would stop.

It took a lot of courage for her to bring it up, but Mama didn't want to talk about Papa.

"Basta umalis lang siya," Mama said, the irritation apparent in her voice. "Okay na ba yung sagot na yan?" She looked away. "Kumain ka na nga lang," she said softly.

Even I knew better than to ask again.

But the visions did not get any better. It became harder and harder to focus in school. The classroom went dark too often. The cries and shouts that came from nowhere made her feel unsafe. Her grades started slipping. Her friends began making fun of her.

When her teachers called in Mama to let her know she might repeat the year, Mama was furious. "Hindi na uuwi ang tatay mo. Huwag mo na siya isipin. Magpakatino ka na at magaral ka nang mabuti para maging top ka ulit. 'Yan lang ang hinihingi ko at hindi mo pa magawa?"

But she couldn't do it, not by herself, anyway.

In school, they had all but abandoned her, except for one little boy, who couldn't seem to leave her alone. When she blanked during a test, he would slide his paper closer to her. Soon, they were inseparable. Wherever he went, she followed. What he did, she did too. When she had her visions, he said nothing. She began to feel like she belonged somewhere, even though she was never really in control—but neither was I.

Ten years pass. Things haven't gotten any better. If anything, the visions have gotten worse. Still, she follows him around—the little boy who is now her boyfriend. When he says, let's go see my friends, she joins him. When he says, talk to them, she tries, even though they have nothing in common. When he tells her we need to take a little shabu, a little bato, something to pick us up, she does. And for a little while, she feels a little bit happier, more focused, free from the nightmarish visions. On it, she is more talkative with friends. Seeing her like this reminds me of the bubbly little girl with all the questions. The child whom everyone had loved before the visions started. On it, she began dancing to a beat in her own head, clowning around, the life of the party.

But the hit never lasts. We need more. When he tells us we need to stop, we can't believe what we are hearing.

And so I hit him. I push him down. His friends try to pry me off him, but can't. I'm in control now, and I won't go without a fight. I hit him again and again. Until he says, "Okay na. Panalo ka na. Eto'ng bato, pero huling beses na," throwing at me the last of his stash, leaving us for good. One by one, his friends follow him out.

Because we had followed him around for a good ten years, we know where to get more, and what I have to do to provide for us.

The source is a few streets away from our house. We show up without the ex. I express my intentions. The dealer shakes his head and laughs. "Anak ka nga ng tatay mo."

Instead of attending school, I attend to my route, delivering enough to cover the cash we need to return to the source. I keep the rest for myself—and for her, too. I come home after school's out, when Mama expects us to.

One late afternoon we return home to the sight of men surrounding our house. One of them grabs our shoulder, says our name.

I answer as calmly as I can, though I feel beads of sweat form on our forehead, and find it hard to breathe. They've figured it out. They're going to kill us.

They drag us into a jeep filled with a dozen other people. I need to find a way out of this.

We are brought to the barangay, made to line up and wait for our turn, in a space as crowded as the MRT during rush hour. One by one my companions are made to enter a room for questioning. Some make their way out. Others do not.

Six hours later, they call us in.

Questions, questions about drugs, if we were doing, if we were selling, why we weren't in school…

Why are we being questioned without an adult companion?

Of course we deny everything. Of course we make up reasons so they would let us go.

They tell us our customers have identified us as a pusher.

We can't go down for this. I take control.

Those people, I say with conviction, are lying. I'm only a 15-year-old girl. I know how horrible drugs are. Doing drugs is disgusting. They taught me that in school.

They seem to believe me. They ask me if I know someone who sells, if I know the name of a pusher.

I pause, then decide that I need to give someone up. If I don't give a name, wouldn't that be suspicious? Wouldn't it seem like I was protecting someone?

I give them the first name that comes to mind.

I say the name of our ex.

I told him to stop. I told him it was horrible for him to sell to others. But he was my best friend, my only friend. The reason why I stayed with him is because he was the only one who would stay with me.

They believed me.

I walked out of the barangay hall telling her I did the right thing. I did what I had to do to protect us. Didn't he break up with us because he thought you couldn't control yourself? Because he thought you were the addict, not him? And yet it was he who had introduced us to this lifestyle.

I had to protect us. It's a small price to pay, giving them his name. He's young, anyway, only 19. They won't do anything to him. They set us free, didn't they?

Let's go home, I tell her. But she says nothing.

I can't face Mama. I know that the neighbors must have told her what had happened.

Nothing.

I thought I was in control, but now I just feel lost.

I have never felt so alone.

I stay low, wander around until nightfall. I come upon a horde of people gathered around a woman wailing in the middle of the street. My heart starts pounding and my chest tightens.

Another raid?

"Kasi naman, ano'ng ginawa niya sa buhay niya?"

"Drugs nang drugs kasi."

"Bakit ba siya nagbebenta?"

I edge around the crowd, frightened to be picked up and questioned again.

But then I hear his name.

The wailing voice, a mother's voice, howling his name over and over.

It can't be. It shouldn't be. I just gave his name a few hours ago.

She makes me turn back, forces me to look at the woman cradling his body, crying and shouting. Blood everywhere. A trampled piece of cardboard nearby. The stamp of the times.

I did that. Not her. I killed our best friend, our only friend.

WHAT DAMAGE

by Christine V. Lao

Illustration by Jewel Tan

Whatever I say won't matter,
not to you. Not even as I declare that bullets
did not end your life, words did.
- Jim Pascual Agustin, "Danica Mae"

1.

: belonging to the same ancestral stock, but not in a direct line of descent—say, brother has turned up, after police detention, his autopsy report still missing; say, cousin was unarmed, begging for his life, before they began shooting, say uncle and buy yourself another day, any which way, we all go down—

2

: relating to, or being security for the payment of a debt or performance of contract—the road to public safety, built on a foundation of lists, the names of all who matter less. Tonight, in certain neighborhoods, someone must die. So enter your houses and lock your doors. Turn off the lights, unplug the security cameras. We need to feel safe so the spectacle must be performed—

3.

a: serving to support or reinforce: as evidence that government is doing its job—as in, We have to plant evidence for the legality of the operation. We are ordered to do these operations, so we have to protect ourselves—

b: as secondary or subordinate to everyday concerns—so that when you say, Your concern is human rights, mine is human lives… to speak of the body (the five-year-old, lifeless, bullet lodged in her neck) is to digress into collateral matters—

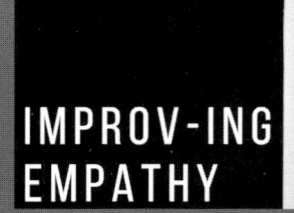

On August 18, 2018, several members of the team joined the "Improv-ing Empathy" acting workshop by actor/director Missy Maramara. The writers were allowed to participate since both the anthology and the workshop were being sponsored by Areté.

The workshop helped the authors learn how to use acting and improvisation exercises to develop their capacity for empathy, broaden their perspectives in dealing with the effects of violence and other unpleasant aspects of human experience. This lesson was key in developing their stories about the EJK, which is a difficult topic for many to grasp.

SEPTEMBER 28

MARCOS, DUTERTE, AND THE IRREDEEMABLE POLITICAL CLASS

September 28

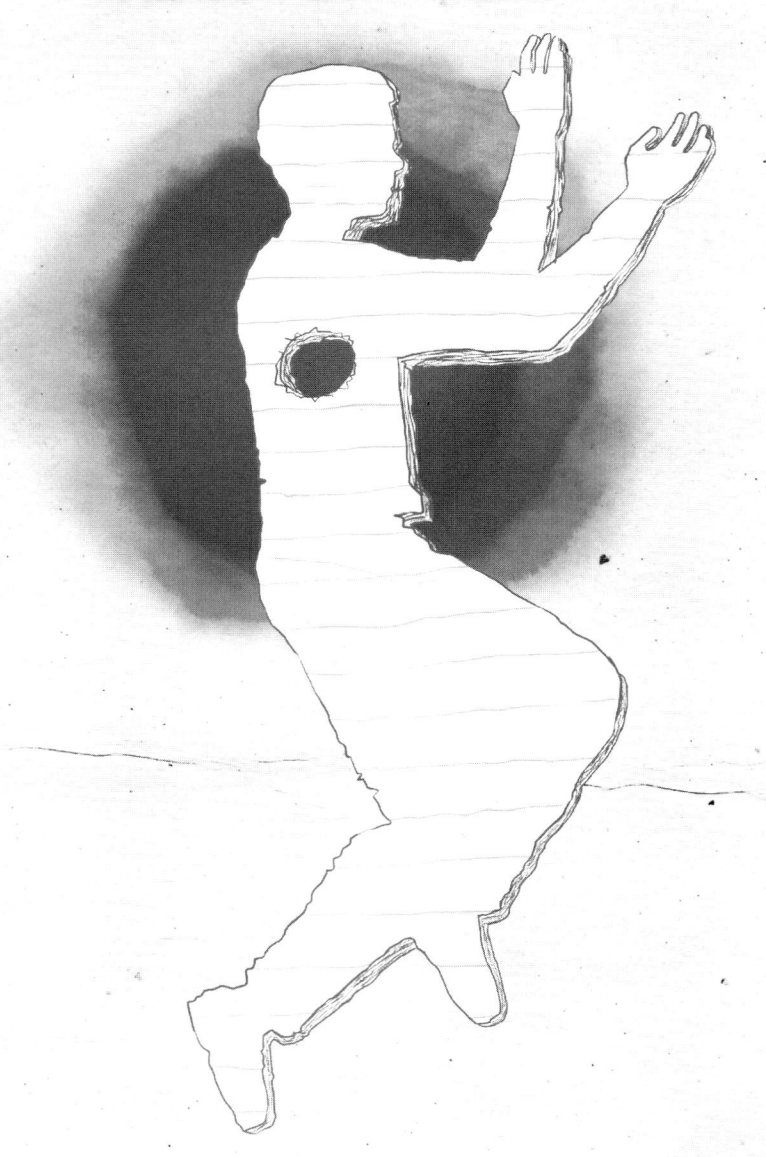

SEPTEMBER 28

by Red Nadela

Illustration by Andoyman

Here's to my good boy, forever my baby Marco.

- *Mommy Mel*

September 11, 2017. 6:05 PM

I am a good boy?

Mommy had told me that when she gave me this journal for my 16th birthday, and I'm not really sure what to feel. What makes a good boy anyway? Is it the belief that what I do is right because of how I've been raised? To be an obedient son and a reasonable friend? Or is it the innocence in every person, long lost but always there? My mom's baby, but how much I've grown already.

Wow, so many ramblings and I don't even understand what I'm talking to myself about. I've clearly never really written before but I guess this could be a start. I'm Marco, 16. Entered UP Diliman just a month ago as a freshman and it's honestly been hectic and I just needed to let it out somewhere. I've been going through fights with my best friend Carlo, really just because we both belong to political families and his happen to be on the losing end right now. He's probably just bitter that his father lost the past elections to mine. Our families never seem to agree on anything. When Carlo and I celebrated my birthday a few years ago, our dads got into a heated argument about something that caused such a controversy. Pathetic, honestly.

Now we've turned into them, these petty fights in the student government or who should be the chairperson of this org or even the whole drug war going on right now that my father proudly campaigned for. It's okay though. We always settle these things and as long as he matures enough to know that I'm right, then we'll be fine.

I know that Carlo's tired of everything I do, from constantly outwitting him among our friends, joking about how badly his dad lost the recent election, and how I talk about my dad's success. Honestly, though, there's nothing wrong with what I've been doing. I'm getting really good grades, my family's bonding better than ever, and it seems as if things are really looking up. This could not have been possible if we were the villain. That's not how the Edralins live out their name.

I knew that, and I chose to live that way for the last 16 years. I am next in line for the dynasty, and I have to act the part.

But Carlo didn't live that way, despite both of us coming from similar backgrounds. I always wondered why, because I always had so much respect for him despite our differences. He actually disagreed with his dad at times, and would side with me, even if it might have been bad for him. It didn't feel like he was this political enemy or rival. There are things I really admire about him, and I don't think that'll change anytime soon. It's really just this stupid political division that bothers me about him, but I'm pretty sure it can be ignored. It's nothing personal anyway, and no one gets hurt. It's just a drug war, nothing more, nothing less. I'm sure everything will be okay.

That's it for me today, I'm really tired and this birthday's been draining. I really love this gift though. I never thought I'd find myself to be quite a lengthy writer. I always preferred being straightforward and concise, but I guess nothing can go wrong with just writing what I really feel. Hands are aching, mind is hurting. Time to sleep.

Marco

September 12, 2017. 6:04 PM

Remember how I wrote that everything was going fine except for this whole fight with Carlo? Well, apparently, nothing is going right because of Carlo. Yesterday in particular was horrible because of this whole drug ordeal thing.

I went to school just expecting the usual routine. Go to Kas 1, learn the same things I've been taught all my life, and just cycle it through with the rest of my subjects. It's nothing hard really, my profs love me because they think I'm smart, and those that don't rarely even went to class so it wasn't a hassle. College life, if it were just about this, would be a lot simpler and I'd have breezed through it already without looking back. Ask me any question about Chem or Math or Kas and I'm sure I'd answer it better than anyone else.

But who cares about grades? Today was really not my day.

I was greeted with a smothering bunch of rallyists in AS, crying foul about my father's alleged anti-poor sentiments, including the whole drug war ordeal that Carlo and I had fought about. Normally, I wouldn't mind. People could never understand the complexity and tradeoffs that politics entailed, and always assumed that whatever is good comes ideally. It's not a pretty sight, but it's reality. I wish they could understand me, or my family, or our ideals. We never intend to hurt anyone, but there are sacrifices that have to be made for the sake of our core principles, like seeking justice for those who are harmed by addicts and making no excuses for criminals. It's about making the Philippines a safer place! But enough about that. Writing won't solve anything.

What really bothered me was seeing my best friend, shouting at me in front of everyone. "Anong pinaggagawa ng tatay mo?!" He stood there, smack in the middle of the crowd. He tried to shame and humiliate me with insults about my apparent lack of a moral compass, an attack on my person and on my dad. I know I'm not a perfect guy, but this was my best friend.

This was the person who approached me on the first day of school way back in Grade 7 and started talking to me despite how shy I was. He knew my reputation, being the son of a politician, too. They treat you differently, they think you're either too good for them or they resent you for the alleged corruption always hurled at all politicians. But he didn't, he treated me like anyone else and gave me the respect I deserved. Carlo came from a rich powerful family like me, grew up in a similar context as I did and no matter how many times we fought, it never meant treating each other like dirt. But now, the pain, the bullying from the same guy. The one guy who I thought understood me was the one guy who hurt me the most.

We had always agreed to disagree. We never let any fights get personal. We never let it get in the way of what was special between us.

But despite it all, I would actually be okay with all that if it was just about me, but he cried foul over my father as well, alleging corruption and his unlawful conduct with the whole drug war. Tarnish my name, but never the man who had sacrificed so much for my family and this country I love. I knew this was all political, and that he really had his own belief, but this hit me personally. I knew he attacked me for the sake of making me feel bad, when I always expected him to understand.

I hope this ends, because despite what happened today, he is still my best friend.

Marco

September 20, 2017. 6:03 PM

It's been more than a week now, and I thought things would be less hostile. But of course that didn't happen. When worse comes to worst, the social justice warriors come in and ruin everything for me. I still didn't care, I feigned ignorance because they would never understand my plight.

Things have been really hard. It hurts to feel like an outcast in my own community, especially when your best friend seems to just love using his influence to make me look like the villain. He'd tweet things like #ImpeachEdralin and #NeverAgain, blaming us for the monstrosities of the past. I expected him to disagree, but I never expected a disjunct that crippled what we used to have. I never expected him to get personal with my family.

This was my best friend, the one I expected to be by my side through it all. This was the Carlo who, on his 13th birthday, brought me to Camp Crame for a special treat. Never had I seen more soldiers with guns by their side, and I couldn't really keep myself calm. Carlo tried to comfort me by telling me he brought me here to face my fear of guns. That in no way calmed my fears, but we stayed at the shooting range and his dad's friends were there. They grew up together since high school, and that was the kind of friendship I wanted with Carlo. I just wanted a normal friendship. What was so hard about that?

Every bang, and every cock of the barrel made me shiver, and Carlo noticed. He held a gun and showed me how good of a shot he already was. Apparently, he'd already been at the shooting range quite a number of times. I was still trembling with the whole ordeal.

He pointed to the gun and it said everything.

It was there on the table. It was black and miniature, just barely bigger than the size of my fist. For me, it encapsulated what it meant to be small but terrible. I held it, but it was shaking in my grasp and my hands were sweating drastically.

"Pasmado masyado," Carlo claimed.

I was irritated but I couldn't deny it.

Carlo came over, and held my hand to guide my aim. He told me to steady myself, and I tried really hard. My finger was on the trigger, but I couldn't bring myself to press it. Carlo opted to push the trigger first, so I could get a feel of it. I let him, and out came the bullet. It was way off, but I didn't really care at the moment.

It calmed me a little, but I was still frightened by the thought of firing the gun. I felt myself steady, closed my eyes, and then I shot the bullet. I dropped the gun almost instantly, and I didn't want to look at the target. Carlo made me face the target again, though. Bull's eye.

Oddly enough, I didn't know what to feel. Carlo explained after that guns aren't really the ones to be afraid of. It's the person holding it. It's the person with the intent to kill. I didn't know if I should've felt happy or afraid. All I knew was that was the last time I was ever going to do that.

Carlo is the guy who knew everything I knew about myself. He knew what I liked doing, my lifestyle, even my fears. This weird, irrational fear of guns, for instance. I never liked talking about them or even seeing them. I hated seeing both of my dad's guns near his dresser. I never understood why, but maybe it was the power the guns gave? The thought of giving the power to kill was just so frightening, and I never wanted that. I explained that to him, and he seemed to understand more than I did.

If our friendship was still like back then, I knew Carlo would've respected me instead of threatening me. I knew all about this drug war and how my dad endorsed it by supporting the different actions that came with it like Oplan Tokhang. I didn't understand where their family would get this absurd idea that my dad was part of that very same drug trade, and how he was apparently abusing his power in the senate to get the drug killings done. The war is just and is not hurting society. That's what my dad always said. If Carlo wanted answers, he could've approached me as his friend.

Marco

September 27, 2017. 6:02 PM

It's been around a week, maybe. Carlo and I, we'd walk the same hallways and our eyes would meet, but the eye contact would never last. One or the other or both would look away, and we'd pretend to be strangers with memories.

I could hear the snickers of our, I mean his friends, and how they'd mock me every time I passed by. I hated going to school, I hated everyone who went to school with me. How could I feel so alone even in a room full of people? It felt so silent and lonely hearing myself think and what they were all probably saying about me.

Then, all of a sudden, one morning he approached me.

"Why in the hell would you allow these innocent people to be killed?"

"Carlo—"

"Do you not care that your father is responsible for this gruesome bloodshed on the streets and the innocents in jail? Have you no mercy for these people around you who could be victimized any time by the police? When will you stop pretending we are living in a time of peace and change, and open your eyes to this red wasteland of hopelessness, Marco?"

"Don't speak to me as if I'm an idiot, Carlo! It's politics! These are political issues with real political outcomes! You cannot just ignore—"

"So why are you letting politics kill people? Marco, I've always been your friend. It's just so weird that you're scared of a gun and how it can kill, but you let this drug war happen and you don't even bat an eye. You're better than that. Can you actually show me then?"

I was shaking maybe for five minutes after he'd left. How dare he talk to me like that. It was a political thing, but it was getting personal and I could feel myself losing control.

The following days it got worse. I felt alienated everywhere. No one in school wanted to talk to me. My family was too busy dealing with political stuff. All my other friends had heard about the allegations regarding my family and stayed away from me. All of a sudden, I became the villain. I felt lost, and all I could find was anger deep inside. I thought I could always rely on Carlo when something like this happened. But he threw away our friendship. He threw away the one thing I treasured with him.

This is my best friend. Or was. To bully me and to shame me for my beliefs is one thing, but to bring hatred and anger against my father, the one person I idolize more than anyone else in the world, that does it for me. To spread these lies of his corruption and alleged involvement in the drug war, it sickens me that I was friends with such a liar and a backstabber, an enemy.

Still feeling restless, I invited him to my house about a few days ago so we could talk things out. Maybe we can still patch things up if I talk some sense into him. Sure, I'm angry as hell, and sometimes I entertain the thought of hurting him, but we are both sensible, reasonable people.

Tonight is the night.

Marco

September 28, 2017. 5:01 AM

I cannot sleep, cannot speak or mutter a word. I hate myself, but all I can do is write, remember what happened, and kill myself inside over and over again.

He was there, he came into my house, just like he used to when we were kids. It was dark inside the sala, and I was waiting for him there. He found the light switch, and found me standing right beside him. I had my dad's gun, to show him I wasn't scared of this power anymore and held him at gunpoint in his chest. Right then and there I must admit I wanted to shoot him, if only to knock some sense into him, but—

I needed answers. "Why would you do this to my family and me? Why would you bully me?"

He kept answering the same thing. He kept saying he never wanted to hurt me or anyone in my family, but that my family was responsible for the thousands of deaths that have occurred in this drug war. He was tense, I could feel it.

"And I never wanted to bully you Marco, that was never my intention. I'm sorry for the times I made you feel alone, and I admit I was a terrible best friend in letting my anger get the best of me. I am so sorry, and you have a right to be mad at me. But what your family is doing— I can't just do nothing."

My hand that was holding the gun started to shake in spite of myself. He probably noticed because he regained his composure and looked at me for the first time. I couldn't help but admire him.

I pressed the gun more firmly into his chest. "Enough about me. Why would you disrespect my father?"

"What disrespect? I only said what I saw. I would never, ever lie or fabricate anything about your father. He's overseeing this entire thing. Are you blind to the deaths?"

It was at this point, I remember, when I heard the stairs creaking, but I didn't pay attention to it. I should have.

"You've already said it, but why my father?"

"Because he's the one who can change things, and it's for the good of everyone."

I felt my breathing slow down and my body relaxing. My hold of the gun loosened.

"Why aren't you scared? I'm about to shoot you and you're not even shaking."

"Of course, I am," he replied, "but some things you just have to do."

I could not bear to hold the gun anymore. I felt water welling up in my eyes, and so many things running in my head. How did I feel? Instant regret for my rage. I kept saying sorry. I pleaded and fell to my knees. He helped me stand up again.

We approached each other for a hug, and we shook hands after. I said sorry for threatening him, and he said sorry if I felt that I was being alienated. He said he meant no personal disrespect to my father. He never intended for that to be the effect. We almost left my house as better people.

Almost.

From some distance behind Carlo, I saw my dad standing on the stairs, and in his hand his other gun.

The last five seconds of that moment keep replaying what I wanted to happen, as if on loop.

One second in. I spot my dad raise his gun, I stare back at Carlo.

Two seconds in. I point to my dad, and Carlo turns around.

Three seconds in. My dad fires the gun.

Four seconds in. I push Carlo out of harm's way.

Five seconds in. The bullet hits me.

None of that happened. I stood motionless. I was scared. I was shocked. My dad shot Carlo right in front of me.

In my head I asked God why not me instead, as his blood spattered right onto my clothes, and he held on to my shoulders. He seemed to beg as he fell to the floor, blood spilling quickly. I didn't know what to do.

I was stuck in my train of thought. Carlo was a good guy, and I wasn't. I let this happen to him, and I cannot believe I ever put him in this situation. I did not deserve to be the one standing tonight.

"Nakikialam kasi eh," my father muttered under his breath. "Parang tatay niya."

He called in the surrounding bodyguards and took Carlo someplace else.

It kept coming back to me, and I could never let go of it. All I could think about up to now was what my father and I did last night. Carlo, laying lifeless, at the hands of my father whom I no longer knew. This was my fault. This was my fault and I cannot blame anyone else.

Carlo lay there lifeless on the floor, eyes closed with his bloody clothes. The bodyguards dragged him away as if this was their routine. Here lay my friend who I knew hated the system I supported, and he had to die for me to realize how naive I was. It was a death in vain, and I should have died instead. All I can think about was the selflessness and commitment he had displayed. It wasn't even him being a De Castro anymore. It was just Carlo being Carlo.

That Carlo died, along with the hope I had of ever fixing our friendship.

I'm still an Edralin. I lie, I cheat, I steal, and I make people believe that I'm good.

To everyone else, I'm a good boy. To my mother and my father, they will always think of me as a good son. I know better.

Marco

"When we had the focus group discussion about our stories, originally I thought the project was to change minds. I kinda realized it was too idealistic. It's hard to change minds even as a professional writer. Even if you make many factual, historical books people may still doubt them, still believe fake news or things like that. It's really hard to change the minds of stubborn people. So at the very least I just wanted to tell a story. And I wanted to make sure this was something that would come out with a perspective that goes deep and is a perspective that people will see. What happens after that, that's not in my control anymore. What one gets is a very individual interpretation more often than not. So whenever I talk about my story, I really refrain from telling people my interpretation of the story. I simply tell them, 'Oh, this is what happens, and this is what happens...' But nothing more, nothing less. Because I want to make sure that everything is up to your imagination."

Red Nadela
on writing his story "September 28"

MARCOS, DUTERTE, AND THE IRREDEEMABLE POLITICAL CLASS

by Glenn Diaz

Image by Nicolai Maverick

When I found myself in one of the many mobilizations that exploded following the news of the dictator's burial at the Libingan ng mga Bayani, I remember thinking how strange to be chanting "Marcos Hitler Diktador Tuta." In 2016. Among millennials. With the towers and traffic of Katipunan around us. It was a chant we learned in history class and educational discussions, immortalized in the iconic Pete Lacaba poem, with a rare force only history can summon. It was a fight that had been won.

We should have known better. The burial came months after the election of Rodrigo Duterte, who had made it a campaign promise. The dictator's family, who left the country in disgrace just 30 years earlier, has long been back in the political fray, his only son and namesake almost winning the vice presidency. Loyalists abound in the bureaucracy, including, as it turned out, the solicitor general and the president of state-run University of the Philippines. The corpse in Batac had not been completely dead after all.

Dead are the thousands of suspected drug pushers and users, the bystanders whose most terrible sin was being in the wrong place at the wrong time, the dozens of children like Kian Delos Santos and Danica Garcia, part of a generation forever scarred by the pitiless sight of bodies splayed on bloodied pavements.

There are affinities between the Marcos and Duterte regimes, of course, some more obvious than others. Fascism cannot help but resemble its iterations because of their broad reliance on unsophisticated force: as in the simultaneous corruption and empowerment of the armed forces, the systematic silencing of critics, the bypassing of due process under the guise of wanton patriotism, all orchestrated by a charismatic tyrant.

That the rehabilitation of the Marcos name took off under Duterte no doubt speaks of a well-planned collusion, an I-scratch-your-back-you-scratch-mine deal that is part and parcel of Philippine politics. Duterte's campaign, touted as a grassroots movement, was after all partly bankrolled by the Marcoses' plundered largesse. A few times he had proclaimed his preference for Bongbong to succeed him. He described Imee as one of his "few allies" in local politics and once waxed nostalgic about his father standing by the dictator during "his darkest hours."

But there is also a danger in simplifying the figure of Duterte as Marcos incarnate. As his landslide victory is seen as a repudiation of his successor Benigno Aquino III's elitist governance and neoliberal policies, substituting Marcos for Duterte is certainly seductive. But it also runs the risk of conforming to the well-worn Marcos vs Aquino narrative, which threatens to valorize a brand of politics that the people only recently rejected. Worse, the bitter fighting obscures the complex relationship between such brand of politics and the plight of Filipinos.

What it obscures is this: that up to 80 percent of our elected officials come from entrenched elite political dynasties, from Ilocos to Davao, that the country's wealth is concentrated among a handful of families, and that these two groups' interests often intersect, all while a huge segment of the population remains poor.

The analysis of political figures then is crucial only insofar as they illuminate the systemic ills that plague Philippine politics, only if in dissecting them we arrive at the feet of this country's greatest traitors: a political class that has, since time immemorial, turned its back on the people whom it claims to serve.

Here is perhaps how "Marcos Hitler Diktador Tuta" gains renewed currency, a reminder that history undulates not with heroes and presidents but with the sheer force of peoples' struggles, that dictators and strongmen come and go but the people's movement persists.

Areté organized a special panel discussion to analyze the stories of the student writers. It aimed to provide them with additional feedback on their stories and insight from experts in various fields such as political science, journalism, and even theater. The meeting was held on February 16, 2019 at the Creative Co-Lab room at the Areté.

The panel consisted of Martin Villanueva (Fine Arts Department Chairperson), Guelan Luarca (theater artist/translator/writer), Gino Trinidad (Political Science professor), John Nery (journalist/editor from the Philippine Daily Inquirer), and Niño Leviste (IPC, SA).

The feedback from the panelists not only gave the writers new insights on their individual stories, but it also challenged the team's perspective on the entire project itself, pushing the team to really expand on the goals and scope of the project.

BAPTISM BY FIRE

ANGEL OF SHADOWS

BAPTISM BY FIRE

by Jan Ong

Illustration by Crisostomo D.

'm not a bad man, I just want to do what's best for my country.

I always believed that every citizen wanted the best for their country. Most wanted it enough to hand over the throne to the swiftest person who could obliterate corruption and sweep up the crime-ridden state in a snap. Even if it meant bloodied hands.

I've been in the Philippine National Police for two weeks now. Some may think it's crazy, but I think that maybe, just maybe, one good soul could make things better.

My walk home every day fueled that burning passion for change. I would pass by narrow crowded streets whose dim lamp posts flickered frequently, the waning light only enough to keep half of the dark asphalt lit. The streets continued to remain busy despite the murmurs of the latest tragedy. Parents shrieked at their children to go back inside their tiny tin dwellings as a blanket of fear clouded the area. The strong winds often buffeted the area, shoving its residents around, the sound of their quick footsteps lost to the maelstrom. The air had a certain heaviness to it, its gravity crashing down on people. The chaos encapsulated each and every individual as they rushed to get their own errands done before the fleeting colors of the sun faded. One could tell by the dark circles under their eyes and the growing wrinkles on their foreheads that this wasn't how they imagined change would come. Change was not a strong, armored knight who would sail across a sea and journey the scorching desert to reach his goal. Yes, change was still strong, but instead, he was a giant that took large and quick strides to finish the race without wondering how many he had stepped on along the way. In an instant, nothing was ever the same.

Maybe it was time for someone to become a knight, just like how he was.

"Jude, kamusta naman ang trabaho mo?" my wife, Joy asked, "siguradong matutuwa ang tatay mo kung puwede niya lang ikaw makita ngayon."

"Ayun.. nakakapagod ang sistema pero umaasa ako na maayos naman ang kakalabasan ng lahat nito."

"Wag kang mag-alala, Jude. Alam ko na kaya mong labanan ang sistema mula sa loob at maging ang pagbabago na kailangan ng ating bayan," she said proudly.

I watched Joy make her way through the rusty, old kitchen door, waiting for her trailing shadow to disappear completely. My wife's soft voice always seemed to echo all the weariness she had been keeping in since my father left us. Despite that, there would always be hint of optimism and sureness in the way she communicated with me. It was funny how my country, the streets, my neighbors, and even the air inside my very own home felt different, yet Joy remained the steadfast rock amidst the churning waves in my life. I let out a sigh that I had been holding in for only God knew how long. Can I really do this? My eyes glanced at the medium-sized picture frame on the cream-colored wall. It was a portrait of my father in his blue uniform. He stood there proudly, his head held high, a glimmering medal affixed on his left chest and a pistol on his hand. The medal was an oddly shaped cross with three stars on each corner, representing his outstanding service in the force.

Yes, this is the right way.

"Ito nga pala yung dropbox, para sa mga takot na residente na gustong magbigay-ulat tungkol sa mga gumagamit ng droga," Juan said as he entered the premise. Juan was one of the Senior Police Officers tasked to guide us rookies. He always wore a mischievous smile that made us recruits uneasy.

When I first entered the force, I heard infamous tales about him. His father used to be one of those shady dealers at the slums who would sell drugs for a rich and influential drug lord. As the police closed in on the drug lord, they planted evidence on Juan's father that made him look like the culprit. Juan grew up with classmates that teased him, saying that his tuition fee was paid by drug money. His anger slowly built up. He was angry at his father for having to take that job. He was angry at the man who saved himself at the expense of his father. And most of all, he was angry at drugs for everything unfortunate that happened to him. Since then, he spent years in the police force, having gone through countless, merciless missions.

Most recently he shot his neighbor's son without hesitation when they found a packet of crystalline substance in his bag. There were those who commended him for what they would classify as bravery, but there were also silent protests going around the community. It was everywhere, in the news, posters, and even in the eyes of those walking in the streets at night. The fear, emptiness and trauma were reflected in people's faces with their aimless movements until the story got buried under the rest of the world's problems.

I examined the chestnut-colored, wooden box that my senior pointed at and lifted it. There were several of these laying around the station. According to him, we had to read through the complaints and note down names for future reference. Today's agenda was all about gathering information to prepare for pending operations.

"O, dapat makalista kayo ng limampung pangalan ah," Juan ordered as he left the room.

"SI RAYMART SIA TAGA NAVOTAS AY ISANG ADIK," Peter, a new recruit like me, read aloud.

I continued to shuffle through the pile of complaints, finding numerous papers filled with threatening and unpleasant words. There were a lot of possible leads. There were some recurring names. There were also times, it felt as if the anonymous tippers were just playing pranks or were fueled by personal grudges, ignorant of the possible real-life consequences that their anonymous "tips" would bring. It was difficult to judge which were genuine tips or not.

PATAYIN SI ROMY MANASIO.

HUWAG TULARAN! MADAMING PUSHERS SA CALOOCAN.

ADIK KA

NAGSHASHABU ANG KAPITBAHAY KONG BADING.

DRUG PUSHER SI RONA SAMSON!

GAGO ANG MGA PULIS

MANYAK, DRUG LORD, AT KABIT LANG SI AGUSTO CRUZ PATAYIN NIYO NA ANG MGA LECHENG GANYAN.

"Paano ba natin makukumpirma kung kapani-paniwala ang mga ito…"

"Basta kunin mo na lang lahat ng pangalan dahil mas mabuting maingat tayo kaysa may makatakas na adik. Hindi magbabago ang Pinas kung hindi tayo matatag sa mga maliliit na bagay na ito."

I followed Peter's advice in spite of the guilt that was welling up inside me. My palms grew sweaty as I listed down name after name of people who might be innocent but will now never be proven so. *Raymart Sia. Romy Manasio. Rona Samson.* Were all these people really involved with illegal drugs? Or were they just victims of foul pranks and angry neighbors? For Peter, it didn't seem to matter. The only thing that seemed to matter here was coming up with a list of people to blame. I watched Peter's face remain unfazed as he went on with the task. He wrote each name with precision, never skipping a beat. A few minutes later, a tall, dark-skinned man in an oil-stained gray shirt entered the room, followed by Juan. The man looked like he was in his late fifties with the wrinkles on his forehead glistening with sweat. He kept shifting his weight between his two feet, as if he couldn't stand still.

"Upo ka diyan," Juan motioned for the old man to take his seat as he turned on the recording device, "ito nga pala ang informant namin sa Caloocan. May tip daw siya tungkol sa mga pushers."

"A-ano po.. Sa may Barangay 160, tuwing gabi, marami pong nagbebenta ng shabu..." His voice would crack after every few words as if secrets were hidden in between those spaces. I suddenly recalled that many of the complaints in the box had names of people from Caloocan. My colleagues used to talk about how policemen would bring in informants when some of their leads were hitting dead ends. The whole police force seemed to be working hard so that they could be authorized to conduct an ominously named "One Time, Big Time" operation, a large scaled anti-drug operation "...kaya yun po, mahilig sila magbenta sa mga estudyante." The man's voice came to a halt bringing me back to the interrogation.

"Salamat ho. Iimbestigahan pa namin muna yun lugar bago kami makakagalaw. Kung may maririnig pa kayong impormasyon, balik na lang kayo ulit," Juan said, as he discreetly slipped a crisp one-thousand peso bill in the man's hand.

"Paki pirma na lang po ng pangalan mo dito bilang patunay sa pahayag mo," Juan added, handing him a pen and what seemed to look like a document with terms and conditions.

The man shoved the one-thousand peso bill in his pocket and took the pen and document from Juan. His left hand quivered as he signed his name. The way he trembled was so subtle that I was almost sure my eyes were just playing a trick on me.

Maybe, it's not wrong. Maybe, the men on the list are really just guilty. Maybe, the old man was really just concerned about the students. Maybe, just, maybe, I'm not just trying to convince myself that this is right.

The next few days were routinary. I'd go through complaint after complaint of "concerned citizens" reporting their neighbors, and sometimes, I'd listen in on shifty characters eager to report the swarm of drug pushers (hopefully for the good it would bring society and not for the bill with each name they dropped). On rare occasions, I would get a glimpse of what the more experienced police officers were up to. Juan with three more officers went door to door in a nearby Barangay the other day to ask drug users to surrender. They came back to the station with a list of citizens for rehabilitation and treatment, but they also returned with a pile of police reports regarding shooting incidents and deaths.

As Juan said, "Hindi talaga maiiwasan na mayroon mga ayaw umamin kahit kitang kita na sa ebidensiya ang mga pinagagawa nila."

It made me wonder what really transpired in those houses that drove policemen to shoot.

On Friday afternoon, the Chief Inspector marched into the station, his head held higher than usual. With a sly smile, he waved a bundle of arrest warrants in front of the small crowd that had gathered to see what he had in store. Whispers and murmurs filled the room and the air suddenly felt like a thousand kilos. In a loud voice he announced that we were finally granted permission to perform a "One Time, Big Time" anti-drug operation in Caloocan. In preparation for this, he instructed that the next few days would be allocated for different tasks such as mapping the area, researching on known drug personalities, collating of arms, target shooting practice, and planning out strategies.

"Ayusin niyo mga trabaho niyo kasi may quota tayo sa OTBT operasyon," the Chief Inspector concluded after his instructions.

"Anong quota? Anong pinagsasabi niya?" I murmured to Peter.

"Serioso ka ba? Di mo ba alam na kailangan ng bawa't istasyon na magkondukto ng tatlumpu hanggang apatnapu na anti-drug operasyon bawa't buwan!"

"Ha? Ganun ka dami?" I whispered as I clenched my fist, engraving nail marks on my palm.

"Oo! Kaya yata gustong gusto nila mag OTBT para matapos na kaagad at mas malaki at malinaw ang magiging resulta," Peter paused, then added,

"Hindi ko pa alam kung totoo pero narinig ko rin kay Juan na…kung mahuhuli o maayos daw natin halos lahat ng nasa listahan nila, may bonus tayo…"

I looked around and watched faces grin left and right. "Kailangan natin huliin o… ayusin lahat sila? Eh yung mga iba dun wala pang lumalabas na siguradong ebidensiya na adik sila!"

An officer behind me laughed and whispered in my ear, "Sus.. Madali lang yan. Buy-bust lang katapat niyan… Tapos siguradong may bonus basta makaquota tayo."

The man's voice sent a shiver down my spine. Buy-bust? What does this officer think he's talking about! In fact, what does this whole police force think they're doing? The anger was building up inside me like a volcano ready to erupt. I felt my blood boil. I couldn't believe that the people around me were so bent on filling their quotas that they would push for such a big operation, knowing that many innocent lives would be endangered. Peter noticed that my right hand was still balled up into a fist. He gently patted it and stammered: "Wag kang magalala, kung ang isang tao ay naging suspek kahit man wala pang panipaniwalang ebidensiyang lumalabas, sigurado ako na kahit konti, may sala din sila dahil wala namang tarantadong magsusumbong tungkol sa kanila kung wala silang ginawang masama."

I bit my lip, fighting the urge to yell at him with all of my pent-up anger. I wanted to do things the right way but I was also too afraid to stand up for myself. My feet grew cold as I looked at the fading nail marks that stung on my palm. Defiance would have guaranteed a far worse punishment for my wife and me. I left the station.

I came home to Joy waiting for me on the porch. All I wanted to do was to fight for my country, but even as a policeman, it seemed like that was impossible. I greeted my wife with a peck on her cheek and entered the house.

"O, musta naman trabaho, honey?"

I stood there in silence for a couple of seconds.

"...Joy, hindi ko na talaga alam kung ano gagawin ko. Alam ko naman na iisa lamang ang layunin naming lahat.. kaso bakit kailangan ganito ang pamamaraan nila?"

I wasn't planning to, but for the next few minutes I found myself pouring all the anger and frustration out on her. I told her about the list of drug users, informants coming in and out with inconsistent stories, people who chose between surrendering or their graves, the drastic quota, and even how I've reached rock bottom for becoming just like them. For a moment, I just wanted to believe that everything they were doing was all for the greater good.

"Jude, hon, relax ka lang," Joy said as she reached for my hand. "Alam ko na bago ka lang at mahirap talaga ang panahon ngayon pero hinding hindi mo kailangan kumbinsihin ang sarili mo na ang paraan lang nila ang tama. Gawin mo ang sa paningin mo ay ang tama. Huwag mo lang kalimutan kung bakit o para kanino ka naging pulis."

I closed my eyes, but my sight seemed to be more vivid than ever. Wailing mothers bathing in dirt at the corner of the street, grieving their lost children. Young girls wandering the night, echoing their fathers' names. An image of my own dad smiling proudly at me, telling me when I was a young cadet that I could do it. My shoulders dropped. To be honest, it was almost as if I had forgotten how my own father looked like smiling. Joy gave my hand a light squeeze and added, "Kaya mo yan! Alam ko na balang araw ikaw ay magiging isang mahusay at kagalang-galang na pulis katulad ng iyong tatay."

What would my dad do if he were still in the police force? He was such a highly regarded cop that I wanted to be like him one day. At this rate, if I didn't start standing up for my own beliefs, would I even live up to his name? I don't think I would even be able to face him at this point.

I decided to talk to our Chief Inspector today. As I marched to his office, I looked around the station that I had been working in for two months. The place looked darker compared to when I first came. The drop boxes that were neatly placed around the station seemed to be messily scattered all over the area. It was as if the lamps that lit the hallways were dimmer, and the white walls that surrounded me were now filled with dirt and soot from the hands of suspects, convicts, and those who had surrendered. I knocked on the door that towered in front of me before turning the doorknob.

"Sir? Puwede po ba kayo makausap muna?"

"Ah, Jude. Bilisan mo lang at madami pa tayong kailangan tapusin para sa operasyon," the Chief Inspector replied.

I took a seat in front of his table. "Sir.. kasi po…sa paningin ko, hindi pa sapat yun impormasyon natin sa mga pushers sa Caloocan eh. Mukhang maraming madadamay na innocente."

I sat there in silence waiting for his reply. He just laughed.

"Jude, bago ka dito, noh? Naku! Madami ka pang kailangan matutunan. Minsan, hindi talaga lahat ng ginagawa natin ay nararapat pero, may mga beses talaga na kailangan ng ating mga kamay madumihan upang mailigtas ang ating bayan."

"Sir pero–" I started to say but he interrupted me, slipping a one thousand peso bill in my hand without even breaking eye contact. It was so natural that it was as if he had done this act many times before. I clenched my fist, crushing the bill between my fingers.

"Huwag kang mag-alala. Lalaki pa yan kapag maayos ang kinalabasan ng ating operasyon," he said. "At dahil bago ka nga pala, ikaw ay isa sa mga siguradong magpapaputok. Kailangan sa mga bagong pulis katulad mo ay madumihan ang kamay upang matuto."

He looked me in the eye. His squinted eyes seemed to flicker in the dark room which made him look like a cat about to pounce on his prey. When the Chief Inspector realized that I wasn't going to respond, he took out a Caliber .45 Pistol from his drawer. He shifted its weight between his hands as he admired the object.

"Alam mo ba kung saan ginagamit toh?" he asked me with a hint of sarcasm as he placed it on the palm of my right hand.

"...sa pagpapatanggol po ng sarili, sir...."

"Maiintindihan mo rin na yan ang pinaka mabilis at mahusay na paraan para ayusin ang ating bansa."

The sight of the gun made time slow down and triggered an influx of memories of my father. The days when he would come home late at night after work with a box of bibingka for us to eat. The time I watched him get awarded for his bravery and service. The picture of him on my living room wall where he held the same kind of gun that was being handed to me, smiling with his PNP Distinguished Service Medal pinned on his uniform.

In this instance, I thought about why I joined the force to begin with. It was to be that one good knight, right? To make him proud? I looked down at the palms of my hands where a gun lay on one hand and money lay on the other. I did do my best to be the change inside this filthy system, but holding these right now, I felt stained. Now, I was just like every other cop out there. I gripped the handle of the pistol and at that moment, I realized that I had chosen to disregard the countless lives that would die in my hands.

I looked around my surroundings and spotted a tall silhouette at the end of the dark alley. The powerful stench of urine overwhelmed my senses. The little gravel and rocks brushed my shoes as I dragged them across the street. As I approached the end of the alley, I noticed that the individual was in his blue school uniform. He was facing what looked like a run-down sari-sari store. The faded posters of government officials and brightly printed advertisements were stuck on the walls. The windows of the kiosk creaked as the boy pulled them to a close. Just like what the Chief said. I just have to place the small packet of crystalline substance a few meters away from his (soon to be) lifeless body. I felt a pang of guilt and stopped in my tracks. I pictured my wife and my father in my head for one last time. I'm sorry.

I continued on with the three other officers following behind me. The target drew closer. It seems like he had just finished closing his shop. I caught a glimpse of the boy's frightened face. I wish that I could've at least gotten his name, that way he wouldn't be forgotten.

I passed by the narrow crowded street where the dim lamp posts flickered, the waning light illuminated half my face. The street continued to remain busy in spite of the murmurs of the latest tragedy where a boy was found dead by a sari-sari store. Parents shrieked at their children to go back inside their tiny tin dwellings as a blanket of fear clouded the area. The strong winds, shoved me around, as I walked aimlessly in this maelstrom. The air had a certain heaviness to it, its gravity crashing down. I could feel the chaos encapsulating me as I walked home after the fleeting colors of the sun faded. Anyone could tell by the dark circles under my eyes and the growing wrinkles on my forehead that this wasn't how I imagined change would come.

I opened the tin door of our house ever so slowly. My wife, who was sitting by the dining table, stood up abruptly at the door's creaking sound and gazed at me. It seemed like she had been waiting for me all night. I swiftly looked away, avoiding eye contact and began making my way to the dining table in slow and painful strides. My heavy footsteps made a muddy trail from the door to the hall. I sat across her while she waited for a few seconds before taking her seat again. We sat there still in silence while the world beyond us went on.

I'm not a bad man, I just want to do what's best for my country.

Illustration by Jon Idago

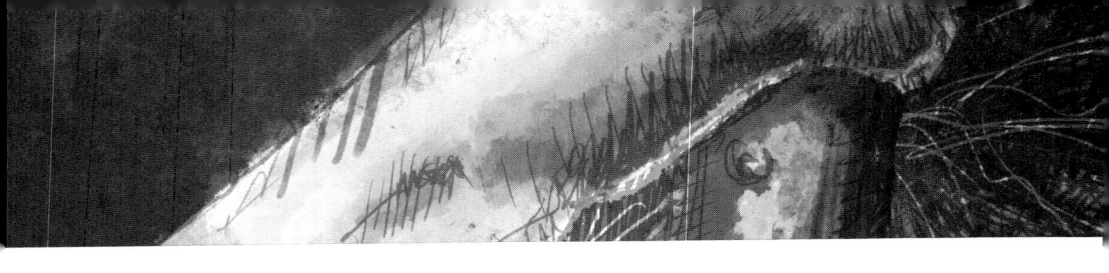

Angel of Shadows (excerpt)
A novel in progress
v06 / April 23, 2019

S he wakes up tired, very tired. As if she spent the whole night wrestling someone in her sleep. Fighting them off, getting them off of her. But she wins. She gets them. They come back, it's always someone else every night. But she wins, every single time.

She goes to the bathroom in the corridor outside. Her body aches. Her back is stiff, as if she'd been carrying something heavy. In her knees a dull, dull ache. A heaviness in her shoulders and arms. She can hear herself suck air into her lungs and blow it out slowly, laboriously. As if she's scraping something out of her throat. Somehow she likes the feeling. Like a good workout. As if she won something. In the mirror she looks as if she slept a lot and needed it.

"Angel, are you awake?"

Mama. What time is it?

"You just got up?"

She tries to speak but can't. Whatever was coming out of her mouth catches somewhere. She coughs, then again. She cups water in her hand, drinks, gargles. She wipes the bar of soap lightly with her hand and rinses her face. A splash of water on her arms then towels it off. She opens the door and sees her mother right in front of her.

"Ma?"

She looks worried, as if her daughter has spent the night out with a strange boy. If only.

"Did you sleep well? There was some noise from your room."

"Oh? Just a bad dream, Ma."

"You still have them, hija?"

"They never left."

She doesn't pry. She understands. If your daughter is nearly raped you're not surprised the memory comes back to her every night when she tries to go to sleep. Nothing needs to be explained.

Angel shuffles off to the kitchen. She takes a plastic food cover off a plate. Mama made longganisa and egg for her.

"Come eat."

Three months and she still isn't used to her own mother making breakfast. If she had left and gone back to Saudi where she was for almost a decade and would just chat over the internet, that would be okay. Her memories of her mother being with her in the flesh are few, most of them distant. The visits at Christmas, but not every year. Showering her with presents. Then leaving her with the space that used to be her mother.

But then Papa isn't here anymore. So maybe it's good this way too.

She sits at the dining table and starts to eat quietly. Mama pours her a glass of water.

"You've been getting up late."

Angel turns and looks at the clock on the wall. Almost ten o'clock.

"It's summer, Mama."

"How can you sleep through this heat?"

No answer, just the sound of food quietly being chewed.

"But this heat, it's nothing compared to over there. A desert is something else. Here the stickiness makes the heat bearable. It's hot, but you're wet with your own sweat, so you won't die. Over there you feel like you're being roasted alive."

The electric fan in the corner hums as it pushes warm air around the room.

She spends the day lazily, trying to do schoolwork but giving up.

Sleeping, looking at her phone, then dozing off again. That night she perches herself on the sofa in front of the TV. The news begins promptly at 6:30.

One headline catches her attention: a gruesome murder somewhere in the city. But that's for later. She stays, enduring the pompous broadcasters who have made careers deepening their voices, filling their speech with the sound of their own importance. A sordid parade. Corruption. Lies from the palace. The president's spokesperson twisting himself into knots explaining the president's latest outrageous remarks. Celebrity news. A handsome boy and a pretty girl doing a movie together claim they are merely friends. Commercials for soaps and creams that promise to whiten your skin. Detergent, instant noodles, soda.

Then it comes: the story of a man murdered in his own home. More than twenty stab wounds. Appendages dangling by a thread. His head nearly severed. The floor wet with blood. (Footage of the grisly scene. A bloodied leg protruding from a pixelated torso.) A policeman says the victim was a notorious thief, hired killer, and suspected serial murderer-rapist. They don't know who killed him but assured the public that they would find out, he says with little conviction.

Victim. They called him a victim. Angel's face feels flushed. An evil man is dead, and we are all just a little safer. He was no victim. He got what he deserved. She feels a little giddy. She goes out the front door, into the small front yard. She wants to celebrate, to call out into the street, to let her neighbors know the good deed she has done for the world. We are all a little safer now. Because of me. I have made it safer.

But who would believe it? A fifteen-year-old girl summoning the spirit of her dead father then appearing in the man's room and stabbing him to death with her father's hunting knife, then vanishing without a trace? Incredible. The stuff of bad movies. Or a long, drawn out fantasy series on local TV with a big-breasted woman as the heroine. The villains with villainous looks and sneers and mustaches.

But this is reality. Here she is the hero, and only she can know. Better that way, perhaps. So she can keep doing it. Why not? If I can take one evil man off the streets, why can't I take others? The thought delights her, sends a jolt through her veins. There will be more to come, she assures the oblivious world.

She owes it to her father, at the least. He was a good man, and he became a soldier to do good in the world. Other soldiers rose through the ranks then became generals, and they lived in large houses in posh neighborhoods, and they acted as if they'd forgotten what it was like to be just another soldier. The constant lack of equipment and clothing and weapons. The bad food. The sense that society had forgotten you, took your service and dedication for granted, ate well and slept well while expecting you to defeat its enemies. He told her stories of people who did bad things, all with an edge in his raspy voice.

Why do it, Papa? Why be a soldier then? Because a soldier can do great things for one's country, for one's people. Because a soldier can be a hero.

Once in a while they were in the news, officers who stole, who gave the rank and file inferior boots and weapons in order to pocket huge sums of money. Angel could see the anger in his face, the brow and forehead tightening, the scowl forming. He would look scary. Papa could look very scary, when he was angry. And he wasn't angry often.

He looked sad, sad more than angry, when she saw him, the night she took his hunting knife from his cabinet and called out to him. The night she decided she would shed no more tears for herself, for what she had endured.

He appeared outside her window, a shadow engulfed in dark flames. He looked at her with that weary look he sometimes had, the one he wore when he was tired with the world, tired of trying to be a good father or husband, tired of just trying to be good in a world that didn't seem to want people like him around. The sadness became pleading. Are you sure you want to do this, my dear little Angel? Do you know what this means? If we begin, do you know where this will go?

Angel thought she could hear him, hear his thoughts in her own mind, in her own heart. He was her father, after all. She could hear him, all right. More clearly now than she ever did while he was alive.

She was sure he knew what was in her heart as well. What can I do, Papa? There is so much evil in the world. And I am afraid. I am afraid of the bad people. The ones who would prey on us. What can I do? The shadows swirled around him like tongues of flame.

If you will let me, I can help you. We can do this together. Will you let me?

Yes, Papa.

I cannot do it without you.

We will do it together then.

Good girl.

Then moments later—she wasn't sure how much time had gone by, she felt as if she'd gone to sleep and was having a vivid dream—she stood in darkness. It felt thick, damp, like a sticky afternoon before heavy rain. Something hummed, like background noise. It got louder. Voices. The darkness lifted.

She is in a room. A table with a plastic cloth. A TV. The voices are coming from it. A man in a low chair or bench, reclined, a foot on one knee. His eyes are half-open. A beer bottle in one hand. She studies his face: It's him. He is right in front of me. I am actually in the same room as him. But why can't he see me? She stands there a while, thinking how much she hates him.

"Start with him," her father's voice says inside her head.

He had grabbed her at a waiting shed, put a hand around her mouth, dragged her somewhere behind a wall where the grass was high. He pushed her to the ground, her face down, and fell on top of her.

"If you shout, I will kill you," he hissed into her ear.

He pulled her skirt up. The smell of grass and mud filled her, and she thought she would die. This is how I will die. She tried to scream, but no sound would come from her mouth. Her body was stiff, frozen, as if it had become separate from her.

Shouts. A dog barking. The man ran off, leaving her half-naked in the grass for the barangay tanod to find.

The memory came to her every night in all its vividness. She would wake in tears. How small he looks now. How thin and weak.

The man brings the bottle to his lips. Then his face turns to her. His eyes grow wide. His whole body flinches, as if he sees a ghost.

She realizes there is something in her hand.

"Punish him."

She thrusts the knife into his neck. The knife has no weight, and her arm feels like it isn't hers. She pulls the knife out and thrusts again. And again. He flings his arms about him, trying to defend against the blows. She slashes at them again and again. They drop momentarily, and she lunges into him, burying the knife in his chest. She pulls back then lunges again, the knife in his belly. She puts all her weight and all her rage into her hand and turns the knife. She takes it out and stabs him again and again and again.

Moments later, it feels like a long time since it began, she steps back. He is a bloody, mangled mess. The floor is wet, blood and beer and shattered glass. She looks at the knife. It is wet, dark with blood and bits of flesh and fabric. The hand holding it is not hers. It is larger, a man's, a scar below the thumb where it meets the wrist.

She steps back. The darkness returns slowly, the voices of the TV growing soft. She thinks she hears shouting, voices from elsewhere, behind her, around her. Then nothing. Nothing but sleep.

SELF-PROCLAIMED HERO

THE LIFE PENALTY

SELF-PROCLAIMED HERO

by Katarina Rodriguez

Illustration by Anonymous

Hidden behind the trees, right across the street, I see the family come home to their poorly built house, too small to fit a family of six. I notice my bracelet, which always brings a smile to my face, as I feel the sweat seep through it. It isn't just the searing heat that's causing the sweat to drip from my face and onto the soil. Underneath my black cap and matching black hoodie, my heart pumps with adrenaline from what we are going to do when the sun sets.

I turn to my boyfriend for reassurance, but he can't meet my gaze. I gently grab his arm and ask, "Mahal, is something wrong?"

He snaps out of his trance and pulls away from my grasp. He shakes his head and gives me a nervous smile.

I try to pull at my boyfriend's arm again, "Let's try get closer to the house."

He looks at me nervously, urging me with his eyes to stay right where we are.

"Mahal, we can get a clearer shot if we cross the street," I pull him harder to follow me. I feel him slightly resist but he knows he has no choice.

I point with my finger after we get to the other side. "You see? We're much closer to the motorcycle, to get away in case something goes wrong."

I hit his hand when I notice him rubbing his palms against each other, something he tends to do when he's about to start crying. I try to direct his attention to the house, where we can clearly see the family preparing their dinner for tonight.

"They look so happy together, maybe we shouldn't be doing this," he mutters softly.

I turn to him, irritated that he would think something like that. "What the hell are you talking about?! The father is playing innocent in front of his family! He's hiding something from them and they have no idea."

He starts rubbing his palms together again. "You—you're right, I a-am so sorry."

I gently take his hand in mine. "It's okay, mahal, just always follow my lead and everything will be fine."

The father needed to die in order to understand that dealing drugs was a disgusting thing to do. He was a threat to everyone. He had to die in order to save the Philippines, in order to keep my children safe. What's one man's life to a million others? To the lives of families? Lives of children? Jose, Janina, Benji, and Nikitta…

My children. My life. I would do anything for the four of you. This is for all of you.

What if I kept him alive? The possibility of my children bumping into him, befriending his children, is terrifying. My children put in danger because of a drug dealer? I can't let that happen. I would never forgive myself if I let him slip through. What kind of mother would put her children in danger like that? It disgusted me to watch this man walk about like he wasn't ruining the Philippines. Our president would not have this kind of behavior. If it were up to the president, this man's body would be on the streets, drained of every drop of blood in his disgusting, soulless body. Since our president can't kill every drug dealer all by himself, we are here to help him out.

People don't understand it yet, why we do what we do. But when the Philippines is clear of these repulsive creatures, everything will follow. My family will rise from poverty. Crime will lessen. But most importantly, my children will be in a safer country. Everything will improve. Everything will get better for my family.

The sun is gone and we watch them eat dinner. Rice and corned beef? What a horrible father. Watching him feed his children such cheap food when he has more money hidden, I feel disgusted. What kind of father is he? If I had the money he had, I would be able to take care of my children better. That's why I need to do this. My family needs the money we'll be getting from this. These drug dealers and their selfishness… Good thing my boyfriend does what I tell him is best for the family. All he needs to do is shoot him, like we talked about.

My eyes snap back to the family, as they switch off the lights of their home. I can't help but remember my children as I watch this family cuddle up together on the floor. I notice a little boy scooch closer and cling to his father, who automatically puts his arm around his son. I can't help but smile as I watch the young boy. He reminds me a lot of my little Jose who clings to me every night as I hug him with the promise of protection. And all of a sudden, I feel this drive to prove to my children that I will protect them from anything, even if that means killing.

I turn to my boyfriend and give him the gun. I watch his shaky hand grasp it. I make eye contact with him, trying to mentally tell him to calm down. I put my hand over his, so we are both holding the gun. I try to stop his trembling, giving him the assurance that he needs.

He seems slightly calmer, so I let go of his hand and nod towards the house. I can still feel the nervousness radiating off him but I know he can do this. We've gone over the plan so many times: drive here, wait till dark, kill the father, drive off, then collect the money the next day. Simple.

"I trust you to do this for our children, for our family." I close my eyes as I breathe in and out, thinking of my children and how much we need this.

Inhale, exhale, repeat.

I open my eyes after the sound of a loud gunshot and the shrill scream of the mother.

I exhale, relieved that it's done.

I turn to my boyfriend. Instead, I only see the gun on the ground next to me. Then in the distance I see my boyfriend tripping over his own two feet on the way to our motorcycle. My eyes dart to the house. The father is carrying his child in his arms, trying to protect him with his body.

The good-for-nothing bastard missed!

The mother is on the phone and I can see the father shouting for help, about to run out of the house in complete panic. I notice the neighbors going out of their little houses to see what is happening.

I don't have much time left. It's now or never.

I grab the gun from the soil, my knuckles turning white from how hard I'm holding it.

The bastard had one job.

I positioned the gun. I aim at the father.

I'm scared. What if I miss? What if they get away and see me?

I feel myself lowering the gun, but then I notice the bracelet my children made for me.

I still feel the gun in my hands and lift it up. I inhale as I put my finger on the trigger. I hold my breath and pull the trigger. I stagger back as I feel the gun's recoil all the way up my arm.

I exhale and look at the house. I see the father's hands covered in blood, but it doesn't seem to be his. He is pressing down on something… no… someone.

It's the little boy, laying unmoving on the ground. Blood is spreading out across the front of his shirt and I feel my heartbeat quicken when I notice even more the blood on the floor under him.

Oh my god. What did I do?!

I drop the gun. I run as fast as I can. I maneuver around parked cars. My blurry vision and the dark sky keep me from seeing clearly where I'm going. I can just barely remember the escape route we talked about. I slip on the rocky pavement and I feel a sharp pain.

My hands clutch my throbbing ankle. I try to breathe through the pain. I think I got away. Nobody saw me. I feel bile rise up my throat as I remember all the blood and the lifeless body on the floor.

I stagger home as calmly as I can. I pass by an officer and he looks at me with suspicious eyes, then a flash of recognition comes over his face. He nods in my direction.

I arrive home to my children. I hug all of them, one by one.

Five days pass and my boyfriend hasn't come home. I've exhausted all means, from begging to borrowing money. But without that money we were supposed to make from that job, we're dead. I make my way to the police precinct, to ask for even just half or a fourth of the money. I don't know what else to do.

When I arrive, I take a deep breath and enter. I walk straight to the head of the precinct and knock.

A strong and firm voice booms, "Come in."

I flinch and open the door. My eyes scan the room and they land on a uniformed figure sitting by the desk. He is a tall muscular, dark-skinned man with a hint of a beer belly.

"I didn't get the job done properly, I'm sor—"

He cuts me off with a laugh and says that what I did was just as good as the initial plan. A grave punishment for a grave crime. That drug-dealing father will have to live knowing it was his fault his kid died.

The police chief gives me the money and says, "Took you long enough to come claim your reward."

I take the money, heart racing. Just before I step out of his office he asks me where my boyfriend is.

I stop and tell him that he ran away before we got the job done so I had to do it myself. The look in his eyes hardens.

"Better make sure that idiot boyfriend of yours doesn't rat us out, or else we may have another 'drug dealer' we would need to… take care of," he says with a loud laugh, but there is no joking tone to it.

With my head down, heart pounding, and hands shaking, I walk home to my children… my life.

THE LIFE PENALTY

by Jamie Bautista

Illustration by Arnold Arre

"OK, that's enough!" Jether Bilanan yelled as he pulled the sleek black helmet off his head and threw it to the ground. It landed with a dull thud on the tiled floor of the police station. Jether took several deep breaths before wiping a tear that had streamed down his left cheek.

"I thought you handled that pretty well… considering," Sgt. Neil Magbanta smirked as he pressed a button on the console of a machine that looked like a large black washing machine with a tablet welded on top of it. "I think this was the button he said to tap once you were done."

The two men stood over the unresponsive body of Tonio Manliban, a twenty-year-old boy strapped to a chair with leather bindings.

"So all of my memories of what this fucker did to me, they're going to be stuffed into his brain so he'll feel like he went through them. Is that what's supposed to happen?" Jether asked Sgt. Neil.

"That's how I understood it, Jether," Sgt. Neil sighed as he adjusted his gun holster. "The boy is pretty much a vegetable now. The tech guy, Dennis, said they did something to his brain… sucked it into this machine of theirs earlier."

"That is correct, the memories and subconsciousness of Tonio were downloaded into the Qualialator an hour ago so he should be an empty vessel ready for the procedure," Dennis Varona, a man in a white lab coat interrupted as he entered the police station's interrogation room. He then walked over to Tonio's bound and unconscious form to examine him when he felt the Qualialator's helmet tap against his shoe.

"Mr. Bilanan, why is the Qualialator's mental scanner on the floor? This equipment is very expensive."

"Call me Jether."

"Mr. Bilanan," Dennis continued. "Have you completed the upload of your selected memories to the Qualialator?"

Jether grunted and nodded.

"He almost broke your fancy helmet doing it too," Sgt. Neil laughed.

"Maybe I just wanted this bastard to stay as a vegetable," Jether growled as he looked at Tonio. "He deserves it after what he did!"

"The point of this process isn't to terminate Tonio…"

Before Dennis could continue, Sgt. Neil put his hand on Dennis' shoulder. "Jether's just kidding, Dennis. Let's just go on to the next step."

Dennis shrugged as he picked up the helmet from the floor, lightly dusted it off with his sleeve, then placed it over Tonio's head. He then typed something on the Qualialator's virtual keyboard and a blue light on the helmet lit up. A digital model of Tonio's brain soon appeared on the screen.

"He's all hooked up," Dennis said. "Preparing for memory and subconsciousness upload. Just waiting for your go signal, Sargent."

"Send the boy to hell, Dennis," Sgt. Neil said in a strangely calm manner.

```
<processing memories>
<verifying>
<memoryowner jetherbilanan confirmed>
<verification complete>
<processing subconsciousness>
<uploading memory3456>
<verifying>
<verification complete>
<running>
```

What a day. I'm never doing three jobs in a row again. That last place was huge. And the owner was an asshole, yelling at me over every little thing. See if I ever answer his call the next time termites eat up his rotting wood garden doors again. Whew, it's good to be home.

Hmmm. Better check my credit meter to see if that bastard made the payment like we agreed. Which pocket in my bag did I put that… ah, here it is.

Are you kidding me?! That bastard didn't pay the full amount? Damn him! What, because his stupid dog ran in before I was done fumigating his place? That wasn't my fault! I'm an exterminator. My job is to get rid of animals, not worry about them! Besides, that so-called humane pest control system he wanted me to use is just some scam for bleeding heart rich tree-hugging snobs like him. I've been doing this work for fifteen years. I know what works. If you don't kill off these pests, they'll just keep coming back.

Dammit, I'm going to have to file a non-payment complaint. But these rich assholes always win in the arbitration. Fifth one this month I'm filing. If this keeps up, I'm not going to be able to afford materials, or I'll have to lay off my last project staff. Ugh.

"Daddy! Daddy! You're home!"

Oh, my sweet little Criselle! All the troubles in the world just seem to melt away once I see your beautiful little face.

"Come here, Crissy Bear! Daddy needs a big hug."

"OK! Hee-hee-hee!"

Best feeling in the world. Huh? Joanna? What is she doing out of bed? She knows she has to be resting!

"Criselle, show your daddy what you made with the Mindseye."

"Joanna, why don't you go back to…"

"It's OK, Jether. I'm feeling fine today. Criselle visualized something for me so it gave me extra energy. Right, Sweetie? And she has something for you too."

"Here, put on the helmet, Daddy!"

I'm still not sure Criselle should be using that mind-reading gadget at her age. I don't trust them. Why doesn't she draw with pencil and paper like we used to do. And she might ask for her own instead of always borrowing Joanna's. And I can't afford another one. I was only able to get that one second-hand from...

"Look, Daddy! That's you fighting all the bad bugs hurting all the people. And you're friends with all the people and the good bugs like butterflies and ladybugs are there cheering for you!"

"Criselle told me she thought of that image because you told her the other day about your work. Right, Sweetie?"

"Aw! That's beautiful, Crissy Bear!"

I have to admit, the tech these days is pretty amazing. I have some of Criselle's doodles on paper in my desk, but this image I'm seeing now in my mind is so clear I almost can't believe a child made this. Those cartoon-like bugs, they're almost good enough to be effects in a Hollywood movie! Is that how she sees me? I look so good in this. I should work out more.

I remember telling Criselle about my job. I wanted to explain why I was away from the house so much. So this is what she thinks I do, like I'm some kind of hero. But I'm only doing this for her and Joanna. To afford those expensive new cancer cures. To send Criselle to a great college. I can't let them down.

"Thank you, Crissy Bear. Daddy feels so much better now, just like Mommy."

<end memory3456>
<processing memory 6574>
<verifying>
<memoryowner jetherbilanan confirmed>
<verification complete>
<running>

"It's not your fault, Dad"

"Thank you, Crissy, but I know I could've done more. I could've..."

"You did all you could. You worked so hard to make your business grow so we could afford to get the treatments..."

"But not the real treatments. Not the ones that actually work for Stage 4 cancer because the damn pharma companies are too greedy to..."

"It's OK. At least the treatments Mom did get gave her a couple more years with us. It allowed us to... to prepare for this. She has so many visualizations for us in the Mindseye for us to remember her."

Criselle is so strong. Stronger than me. I'm falling apart here. All of this: the funeral, the flowers, the wake, the food, even talking to everyone, that was all Criselle. Here I am, this big shot entrepreneur and I'm a useless waste while it's the high school freshman who is keeping everything together. And after losing her mother. I'm so lucky to have a daughter like her.

"Hey, Jether. Criselle. My condolences. I'm so so sorry, man."

"Thanks for coming, Sgt. Neil. It means a lot to me and Dad."

"Thank you, Neil. And thanks for helping set up the funeral procession tomorrow."

"Hey, it's the least I can do for old friends. Do you know how many times Joanna got me out of trouble with my wife over the years? I'd close down the whole town for her if I could."

"Oh, that's our insurance agent. I have to talk to him about the coverage of our memorial plan. Excuse me, Sgt. Neil."

I couldn't even cover all the expenses. I kept fighting Joanna about getting insurance, telling her it would be better spent on growing the business. Of course she was right in the end. No wonder she left Criselle all the details about it.

"How are you holding up? I... I can't imagine what you're going through."

"I still can't imagine it, Neil. It hasn't... sunk in yet, you know? Sorry, I don't think I can talk about..."

"No, no, it's OK. Sorry, my bad, man."

"I'm just so lucky I have Criselle here. I'd be so lost without her."

<end memory65674>
<processing memory8965clg>
<verifying>
<memoryowner jetherbilanan confirmed>
<verification complete>
<running>

"I did not pay millions of pesos for your college education for you to become a... a crisis counselor?! Does that even pay? Can't you just do that like on the weekends or something?"

"So what did you pay millions of pesos for me to become, Dad?"

Criselle's giving me that look again, like I'm some selfish stubborn old troll who only cares about himself and his own. She has too much heart, but I've coddled her. She doesn't know what it's like out in the real world, to fend for yourself. And I won't always be around. I have to put my foot down. The blood is rushing through my head and I grip the edge of her bed as the two of us sit on it together, trying to keep my voice calm.

"To become someone who can survive! You can't help people until you can help yourself first, Crissy. You need to do well then do good."

"Can't I do well while doing good?"

I have to stand. I think I'm not getting my point across to her strongly enough, sitting here on her teddy bear print comforter. She has a home court advantage since we're talking here in her room. Of course she decides to tell me this here. Does she even know how many strings I had to pull to get her those job interviews which she just conveniently "forgot" to go to? She has no idea how the world works!

"You think I was able to build my extermination business by being nice? You think I loved inhaling toxic gasses and wading in dead roaches every day when I was starting out because I wanted to help humanity? No, it was the opportunity I had at the time and I took it. And after years of working hard at that, now I'm successful and I can give to charity and be socially responsible, and do all that stuff. But you think the business could have stayed afloat if I gave money to charities when we had so little of it ourselves? Or if I couldn't compete on price if I had spent on those expensive humane and environmental pest control systems clients said they believed in but weren't willing to pay for? Sure, now I can because I can afford to do all that. But I couldn't at the start. You need to face the harsh realities to survive first. So you can do all you want to help society and all, but that comes after you take a job that will help you survive on your own first."

I'm yelling already. I need to calm down or she'll just shut me out. But she's looking at me with that warm smile that could melt icebergs. Huh? I was expecting her to yell back at me, to fight me on this. She's never been afraid to argue with me on things.

"Dad, I get it. And I love that you worry about me. But what about we work as a team? You worked hard for our family to do well. So that is now what's going to allow me to make our family do good. There are so many people out there going through so much, that have the world against them, that don't have the love and support I was always so lucky to get from you. So I just want to give that back. I think that's what you spent all that money on me for. Isn't that OK?'

She really is too good a person. And she's also too smart for me.

"Of course it's OK. But I won't always be able to..."

"I'll find a way to make it work, Dad. I can fend for myself. I know I can make it because you taught me how to survive, gave me all I needed. And I trust in you. Don't you trust in me?"

Before I can even make a sound, I'm already hugging her as tight as I can. I know I'm going to tell her I trust her, but deep inside I feel this urge to never stop embracing her, never let her leave my side.

"Of course I trust in you, Crissy Bear. I just... You know I'll never stop worrying about you."

"I know. It's why I love you so much, Daddy. But you have nothing to worry about."

<end memory8965clg>
<processing memory986767mrdb>
<verifying>
<memoryowner toniomanliban confirmed>
<verification complete>
<running>

Did I remember to get everything for dinner tonight with Criselle? I shouldn't be this excited, but we haven't had dinner together in two weeks. She's been living on her own for two years now, I should be used to it by now. But I can't help it. Any time she comes to see me at home feels like a big deal.

Let's check the old cell phone.

Crissy always teases me for not just using the holo-mental checklist app on my Mindseye. It's always connected to my skull now, as she keeps saying. We've come a long way from that old version of Joanna's that we used to have to wear.

But call me old-fashioned, I still like to use my hands to check off my to-dos. I like the feel of good ol' glass and LED under my fingers. I mean, if we can't use our hands while traveling, why did they invent auto driving cars in the first place?

OK, I've got the wine. Already made the call for the Thai place to deliver the green chicken curry and phad thai noodles. Got her favorite ensaymada rolls for dessert. Have those papers about the car's registration I need her to sign. And that checks everything off!

Oh, damn, I forgot my bag at the office! I guess if it wasn't on the checklist... My memory really isn't what it used to be. I'd better tell the car to turn around and drive back to the office first. I should call Crissy to tell her I might be a bit late.

She isn't picking up her Mindseye. That isn't like her. I'll try again.

Still nothing. It's been ringing for over two minutes now. Is she still at the rehab center? She was supposed to be done by now.

Wait, what's that? It's a Mentalnote from Crissy. I didn't notice that earlier. Another thing Crissy keeps bugging me about: turning on my notifications. But I can't take the constant buzzing in my brain so I mute everything except calls. It was sent about an hour ago. Let's see what this is. Why would she send me a note when we're going to be seeing each other tonight?

What is this? It's like a jumble of fuzzy mental images. Criselle's Mentalnotes are always so crisp and clear.

That looks like the visualization she did for me when she was a kid. That's me and Joanna in the audience clapping for her during her first elocution contest win. That's me with her at her high school graduation. Me hugging her during her college graduation. Her crying on my shoulder after her first break-up. Now it looks like her when she worked at my office for a few weeks to help out, when we had that long talk. And now it's... my face? What's this now? I can't make it ou... Are those her hands? That's... That's blood!

Call her! Call her now! C'mon, Crissy Bear, answer your Mindseye, please! Please!

Oh no. That notification. It's an emergency signal from Crissy's Mindseye. No. No!!! Please, no! Oh God, please no!

The GPS coordinates are pointing to the rehab center. Tell the car to go there now!

```
<read error>
<bad blocks in memory986767mrdb>
<read error>
<bad blocks in memory986767mrdb >
```

```
<skipping>
```

It can't be her. That's not her under that sheet. It caaaaaaaa——
djlhushlsjrht

```
<read error>
<bad blocks in memory986767mrdb>
<read error>
<bad blocks in memory986767mrdb >
<upload paused>
```

"What's happening to the boy?" Sgt. Neil asked as Tonio started to convulse, drool dripping down the side of his mouth. Dennis tapped wildly on the Qualialator's screen.

"One of the memories Mr. Bilanan chose to upload is probably corrupted. It's not syncing properly with Tonio's brain," Dennis blurted out, his eyes not leaving the screen.

Jether's eyes widened and stomped towards Dennis.

"Are you saying this is my fault?! Why doesn't your fancy mind reader machine just pick memories from my mind that it can work with?!"

Sgt. Neil grabbed Jether's arm. "Calm down, Jether. Dennis isn't blaming you." He then turned to Dennis, who was cowering behind the machine. "Isn't that right, Dennis?"

"Y-Yes," Dennis stammered. "Sorry, I wasn't trying to imply anything. It's just that this tech is pretty new, so we're still figuring out all the bugs. That's why this is a pilot project. The machine can't just pull out raw thoughts or memories, at least not in any format the human consciousness can comprehend. Like I tried to explain to you earlier, Mr. Bilanan, it can only read and copy thoughts you willingly bring up to your conscious mind, like with a Mindseye."

"So what's wrong with that memory I brought up? I've shared that memory with people via Mindseye before. Neil has seen it!" Jether yells back.

Dennis nervously adjusted his glasses. "But the Qualialator doesn't work like a simple Mindseye. It doesn't just project mental images or memories into another person's mind. It has to make the receiver believe that the memories they are getting are their own true memories. There's a concept called qualia, which is where the machine gets its name. It is the idea that mental states like perception, sensation, thoughts, and emotions all have a subjective feel to them. It's why you can, for example, do exactly everything your friend did at a vacation, yet still have an experience that's unique from his."

"So it's basically like the saying, 'You had to be there,' right?" added Sgt. Neil.

"Precisely!" Dennis replied, an excited smile coming over his lips. "There's a gap between knowledge and experience. It's why you can know everything about a person, but not quite know what it's like to be that person. Writer John Gardner in his book *The Art of Fiction* calls it 'psychological distance'. It's the space between you as a reader and the character, or how close you get into the character's head. That distance is never quite zero as you're always still aware that you're… you."

Dennis placed his hand gently on the Qualialator's chassis like a mother caressing her child. "But the Qualialator bridges that distance and overcomes the concept of qualia by not just showing you someone else's memories. It makes you believe you are experiencing those memories as that other person. It does it via a process called onboarding, where it makes the subject forget who they are during the procedure so they can take on the identity of someone else whose memories are uploaded."

Jether glared at Dennis, still annoyed. "I'm not that tech-savvy, boy. I still don't understand what the hell you're saying. Speak plain English!"

Dennis nervously fixed his glasses as he tried to explain things to Jether again. "You know how old word processors worked a few decades back, right? Before mental UI? It's like we cut and pasted Tonio's memories and subconsciousness first into the Qualialator's internal storage, leaving his brain like an empty file. Then we copied and pasted your memories and subconsciousness into it. This way, Tonio thinks he is you. But your recorded memories need to be properly synchronized with your copied human subconsciousness to achieve full empathy and to properly bridge the psychic distance."

Jether shot Dennis a dirty look. "Again, speak plain English. So what's faulty? Is it the way I picked my memories or that damn machine?"

Sgt. Neil walked over to Jether and shrugged. "Dennis is just saying we don't know. He's figuring it out. Look, this is all new to everyone, so let's just give the process a chance."

"Why? Why should we give it a chance? Why should we give him a chance?" Jether glared at Sgt. Neil while pointing to Tonio's prone body. "He's a killer! He killed my Criselle!!!"

"Do you really think pumping his head full of my sad memories will make that bastard a better person?"

"Based on earlier test runs done in the U.S. and Europe, the procedure should result in Tonio being rehabilitated," Dennis held up his hands for Jether to stay back. "In theory, after the procedure, he will be himself again but he will have clear memories of being you in those moments you chose to upload into him. And he should have the same emotional responses to those memories due to them being linked to your subconsciousness that was also temporarily uploaded into him. So he should theoretically repent and have the desire to make up for the crime he committed."

"In short," Sgt. Neil added, putting his hand on Jether's shoulder to calm him down, "everything you wanted this boy to feel... the anger, the hurt, the emptiness, the love you had for Criselle... he's going to feel it and remember it exactly the way you did. Basically, he's going to have you in his brain 24/7, never making him forget what he did."

Jether looked back and forth between the two men, then gave out a loud sigh of resignation. "So what, you need to plug me in again and give you another horrifying memory? Look, I don't know if I can go through bringing up that memory again. I can barely remember anything from that night. I-It's like I was in a daze after I got the alert."

"That's probably it," Dennis said as he pointed to Jether before quickly turning back to type on the Qualialator's touch screen. "The emotional trauma of those memories must have degraded them. OK, I think I can make some adjustments to the algorithm so the system can bypass the synchronization with any unclarified memories, so you won't need to upload the memory again."

"This is going to work, Jether," Sgt. Neil said, smiling gently. "You've set things up. Now Tonio's going to feel the pain he caused you."

"All set, I'm going to resume the process now," Dennis called out as he pressed the touch screen.

<resuming upload>
<bypassing bad blocks in memory986767mrdb>
<processing memory986767mrdb>
<verifying memory986767mrdb>
<memoryowner jetherbilanan confirmed>
<verification complete>
<running>

It can't be her. That's not her under that sheet. It can't be.

"Mr. Bilanan? I'm sorry but we really need you to identify the body."

Dammit, don't rush me, lady! I'm sure you and all the other doctors like you are used to seeing dead bodies all the time. I bet you forget that these were people. These are people!

Please. Don't make me look under that sheet. I want to just stay in this moment, where Crissy might still be alive. There's a chance they got the wrong person and somebody else's daughter is under there.

"I'm sorry, sir. I know no one is ever ready for this, but it's part of the protocol."

She's pulling off the sheet. I can't look. I want to just drown in the darkness. But I can't keep my eyes shut forever.

Oh god. Oh god!!! Dhldhlkhkzzzzz8ddhhskn——

<recalibrating>
<running>

"K7bd45sklhe...leave and give you some time alone, Mr. Bilanan."

She looks like she's just sleeping. Her face is so peaceful. But I don't want her to be peaceful. I want her to yell at me for being so stubborn. I want her to cry and hug me and beg me to tell her things will be OK. I want her to laugh so hard soda comes out of her nose like she does when we have dinner out. I want...

The coroner lady didn't pull the sheet all the way down. Thank god. I don't want to see the stab wounds. They said... Her hands had wounds so she put up a fight. I don't even remember... I don't want to remember how many times she was...

Why, Crissy? Why did you have to stay late all by yourself? I told you that center wasn't safe, with all those fucking addicts and criminals coming and going through its doors. You never listen! It was just one drugged-out maniac trying to get into the center at night to... Why didn't you just run? You told me you knew how to handle yourself!

At least they caught the bastard. But those idiots at the rehab center should never have let Crissy walk home alone! Their fucking security only came around when he was already... when she was...

You were too good for this world, Crissy Bear. That's the only reason I can think of why an asshole like me is still on it and you're... you're...

God, no. My Crissy Bear...

No...

AAARRGGGGHHH!!!!

Fuck. My hand's bleeding. I shouldn't have punched the wall.

I'm sorry, Crissy. I know you hate it when I lose my temper. You get mad when I get mad.

Can you get mad at me? Can you get mad at Daddy please? Get up and scold me, please?

Please, Crissy Bear? Please...

God...

<end memory986767mrdb>

<finishing upload>

<memory loop completed>

"Memory loop is complete," Dennis declared as he checked the display on the Qualialator. "And it looks like he has achieved full bridging of the psychic distance." A single tear dripped down out of Tonio's cheek.

"So, Sarge, when do we start the reintegration of the memory loop with Tonio's original memories?" Dennis asked Sgt. Neil as he wiped the tear off Tonio's face before adjusting his headset.

"Give it a few hours," Sgt. Neil replied curtly. "Let him have Jether's memories stew in him for a while. To make sure they stick. Maybe give him some extra nightmares down the line, right?"

"That just sounds like being cruel out of spite," Dennis muttered to himself. "Rehabilitation is what this system was designed to..."

Sgt. Neil suddenly grabbed Dennis by the arm, glared at him, then slightly tilted his head towards Jether. "I don't think this is the right time to talk about stuff like that, OK?"

Dennis quickly glanced over to Jether before he sheepishly smiled back. "O-Of course. Don't listen to me. You know us geeks, we just like to wonder about all sorts of crazy stuff. Most of which is nonsense! Heh. A-Anyway, I should go and submit the readings we've been getting from Mr. Manliban for the evaluation." Dennis nervously fumbled with the door for a few seconds before awkwardly stumbling out of the room.

Sgt. Neil sighed then turned to his old friend. Jether stared silently at Tonio, watching the boy's face twitch and grimace as memories... his memories... ran through the young man's brain.

"Thank you for agreeing to be a part of this program, Jether. I know how hard it—"

"You don't know," Jether interrupted without moving, his eyes still focused on Tonio.

"I'm sorry. You're right. I don't know. But he does now," Sgt. Neil said as he gestured to Tonio. "He feels the exact pain he caused you. And I hope... I believe it will change him, so he can make up for this awful hole he left in the world. And that's the only way I think real justice can come about. I hope you see that too."

Jether continued to look at Tonio, his expression disturbingly blank. "I just... Can I just have a minute alone with... Can I have a moment alone here? I just need to gather my thoughts."

"I can't do that," Sgt. Neil replied bluntly.

"But I thought that's why you let me be part of this! So I could get close enough to…"

"Sorry, Jether. You misunderstood. I wanted you here to stop you from killing the kid."

Jether shook his head and laughed. He then glared at Sgt. Neil. "How are you not more angry at him?" Jether asked, his tone still strangely calm. "I remember that day at the station when you told me about Criselle. You told me you wanted to kill him."

"I didn't mean I was actually going to kill him."

"You telling me you weren't angry?"

"Of course I was! I still am! But what we're doing here isn't about anger, it's about justice!"

Jether slowly turned around and looked Sgt. Neil in the eye. "So you really think this is justice? Letting shit like him live and redeem himself while innocents like Criselle never get that same chance and just keep ending up dead? That's your justice? See, this is what happens when cops like you become bleeding hearts when they should be working to get rid of the vermin of society."

"Here we go again. So what, Jether, you want us to go back to the way it was in the late Twenty-Teens? You always tease me about it, but I know deep inside you mean it. So you want cops like me to kill people without due process?"

"Yes!" Jether yelled, his emotions finally spilling out. "The regime back then had the right idea! If people back then hadn't gotten soft on crime, then other administrations would have followed and eradicated all those murderers and drug addicts. If we had literally stuck to our guns... I bet there wouldn't be any crime today! But instead, we ended up coddling these killers saying it's all about 'human rights'. Now they don't fear anything! It's only innocent people like us who are afraid! It's people like Criselle who lost their right to fucking live!"

"I was hoping you might have had a change of heart, Jether," Sgt. Neil sighed sadly. "That maybe you'd trust this new system. That you'd trust me to —"

Before Sgt. Neil could complete his sentence, Jether suddenly lunged towards him and knocked him to the ground. Jether tried to grab Sgt. Neil's sidearm from his holster, but the cop wrestled the grieving father, gripping him by the wrists.

Suddenly, Jether managed to swing his elbow, hitting Sgt. Neil in the face and causing him to release his grip. Jether plucked the pistol from Sgt. Neil's side and scrambled to take a shot at Tonio. But Sgt. Neil managed to land a swift kick on Jether, throwing him off-balance as he fired. The bullet hit the ceiling.

Before Jether could pull the trigger again, his head was struck from behind with a metal keyboard. Jether collapsed face down on the ground, unconscious. Dennis was standing over him, keyboard in hand and beads of sweat dripping down his forehead.

"I thought you were going to convince him to go through the process voluntarily!" Dennis asked Sgt. Neil in a state of panic.

"Well, there are a lot of things we think will work that just don't," Sgt. Neil smirked as he started to drag Jether towards the Qualialator. "This process had better not be one of those things, Dennis!"

"I can't guarantee anything, Sargent! I told you as much when we came up with this plan!" Dennis cried as he grabbed the helmet off of Tonio and placed it on Jether.

"Well, it's too late to switch gears now, Dennis," Sgt. Neil sighed. "Just do your thing"

"A-Alright," Dennis stammered as he started typing frantically on the Qualialator's screen. "Beginning download and temporary storage of Mr. Bilanan's memories and consciousness... Preparing Tonio's memories for upload..."

The helmet's visor gave out a distinct glow as it activated and Jether's body jerked momentarily.

```
<downloading memoriesconsc of owner jetherbilanan>
<download complete>
<ready for upload>
<processing memories>
<verifying>
<verification complete>
<processing subconsciousness>
<uploading memory1897>
<verifying>
<memoryowner toniomanliban confirmed>
<verification complete>
<running>
```

"Kuya Tonio! Look! I solved it! I'm so good! Write me another math problem!"

"Aw, c'mon, Anjo. Really? I have to help Ma with so many things before that drunk bastard gets home. You want me to get beat up again?"

Look at him. He looks so excited and so proud of himself. OK, let's see if he got it.

"You got it right, Anjo. The answer was sixty people on the jeepney."

"I'm so good at math! Make me another word problem! Please?!"

I'm impressed. He's only six and he solved that in five minutes. When I was six I don't think I could even read a word problem correctly. OK, I guess I should humor him. Mom says we should keep Anjo excited about learning. The kid's smart. He'll be going places. Not like me. I might not even pass seventh grade. Anyway... word problem. Now where did I leave my old third grade math book? Sheesh, I've been using that thing more with Anjo now than when I was actually in third grade. I wish we could afford one of those fancy Mindseyes so I could easily...

"What are you little shits doing standing around here doing nothing? Why aren't you helping your mother clean our shithole of a house?"

The old man's back from the cock fight. He looks pissed. He probably lost money again.

"Why aren't you helping her clean the house?"

Ow! Why haven't I learned to dodge him? I knew he was going to hit me. My cheek is still sore from the last time he punched me. Why isn't my body as fast as my mouth?

"You shut up, Tonio! I was trying to make us some money! Not like you worthless shits who just cost us money. Gimme that and go be useful!"

No! Anjo's paper! Why is this drunkard so fast?

"Hey, give that back! That's Anjo's!"

Ow! Great. Now my other cheek.

"I said shut up and go help your mother clean! Start by throwing this bit of trash out! I'm going to bed."

Asshole didn't have to step on Anjo's paper. Now it's covered in mud. Anjo's just standing there. He looks like he's in shock.

"Hey. Hey, Anjo. Listen, it'll be OK. Dad's just... tired. Go help mom with the dishes. I have to prepare the load of laundry she has to do for Mrs. Enriquez later tonight. If we don't get that done, we may not have money for electricity tomorrow."

"But my math problem..."

"It's OK. I'll write you a new one later tonight. Anyway, we know you got the last one right. You're a natural math genius."

"OK, Kuya."

"OK, get inside the house. I'll be there in a bit."

I think Anjo's OK. But this isn't OK. Dammit, how do we keep living like this with Dad? Can we run away with Mom? Can we... get rid of Dad somehow? If only for Anjo...

<end memory1897>
<processing memory 196?>
<verifying>
<memoryowner toniomanliban confirmed>
<verification complete>
<running>

"Run, Anjo! Run!!! Go to the plaza! I'll find... ungh! I'll find you there!"

Gotta hold Dad back so Anjo can get away! This was such a bad idea! Where the fuck did Dad get a knife?

"Let go of me, you little shit! Graaaahh!!!"

Agh! Dammit! He cut my arm! He's too strong. He's drunk and moving like a madman! I have to keep holding his arms or he'll stab me, but I can't do anything else! Wait... my legs! Just gotta lift up my knee and...

"Unnggh!!!"

Yes! Right in the balls! Thank God! He's down. Serves you right, you fucker! He let go of the knife! Gotta grab it! OK, got it! Point the knife at him. Show him he doesn't scare you. Now I can get some answers.

"You got some balls on you, Tonio."

"Lucky for me, you do too. Now answer me!"

"You're crazy, boy!"

"I'll ask you again. Did you kill Ma?"

"I'll kill you if you keep—"

He's getting up!

"Stay down if you don't want me to stab you!"

OK, he's backing down. Whew.

"You told us... You told the police she ran away and left us. But all these months, I knew deep inside she would never do that to us."

"You don't know your bitch of a mo..."

"Shut up! I'm the one talking here! I knew she would never leave me and Anjo. Then the other day, I saw one of your shirts had a blood stain on it. I realized I hadn't seen you wear that shirt since the last day we saw Ma. What did you do, old man?!"

"I've told you a million times, she left you because you boys are good for nothing— Arrrghh!!!"

I stabbed him. Oh my God, I stabbed him in the shoulder. I... I couldn't help it. It's like my body just moved on its own. Just... Just keep talking. Act tough. Act like you meant to do it. Oh God, the knife's still in his shoulder. Pull it out!

"F-Fine. Don't tell me. But I know it was you. That's why Anjo and I are leaving. Don't follow us. Don't look for us. If people ask, just say we ran away too to look for Ma. Whatever. Just don't come after us. Or I'll kill you."

Back away slowly. Back away. Now run! I have to head to the plaza and find Anjo. I don't know where we can go, but anywhere will be better than this dump. Oh God, I'm still holding the knife...

\<end memory 1967\>

<processing memory2458>

<verifying>

<memoryowner toniomanliban confirmed>

<verification complete>

<running>

"Kuya, you're home! Hey, guess who got first honors again?"

"Ben Arceo?"

"Funny. But... yeah, he did too. And I would've ranked higher than him in class if Mrs. Montelibano wasn't so biased against me in..."

"Hey, I'm so proud of you, bro! When you graduate next year, you're going to have your pick of colleges! I can already see all the scholarship offers coming in!"

I want to get back to my room. I'm so tired. I need a fix.

"Have you had dinner? Sorry, I got hungry after school so I ate ahead. I didn't know you'd be home so late. And the ref is a bit empty actually..."

"I'm good. I ate at the factory."

Dammit, it's time for groceries again? We already used up all the overtime pay from last week? It's OK, I can let another meal pass. Can't let Anjo worry. But now I really need that fix.

"Anjo, I have to get some sleep. I'm dead tired."

"OK, Kuya. Good night! See you... Hey, something fell out of your bag."

Shit.

"It's nothing. I'll get that. It's just..."

Dammit! He's going to find out...

"Wait. This is one of those hacking chips for the Mindseye, the one that runs on that chemical to send signals to hack your brain. SBX. These are illegal! Are you... Are you using this?"

Shit.

"Look, some guys at the plant let me try it a few weeks ago. They said it would help me with the late nights, so I could keep awake and alert longer."

"Kuya, hacking your brain like that with a Mindseye is dangerous! People get addicted to this! And you need to keep refilling the chip with SBX for it to run. And after a while, your brain learns to filter it out so you need stronger doses to..."

"I know all that. My co-workers have a source who gets it for us cheap. So don't worry about it affecting our budget because..."

"I'm not worried about the money! People who've gotten addicted to this end up having violent episodes! Sometimes they lose sense of who they..."

"Well it's a risk I have to take, OK? I work at a fucking printing press. Do you know how much demand there is for paper things with all this digi-mental stuff around now? But what other company will hire someone without any diploma? This is the fifth job I've had in two years and we can't afford to lose it! They just laid off five people last week and they're only keeping those who can put in the extra hours with minimal mistakes. This chip is the only thing that keeps me ahead of the game there!"

"But if you get caught..."

"Let me worry about that, Anjo! OK?! I'm doing all this for you! So you can keep going to school and beating Ben Arceo's ass in tests and get a great job and pull us out of this dump. Right?"

"Right, Kuya."

I didn't mean to yell at him. I'm just so tired and hungry. I need that hit.

"Give that to me. Trust me, I'll handle this. You just focus on school, OK?"

"Alright, Kuya. As long as you know what you're doing."

Nobody knows what the hell we're doing, Anjo. I'm just playing it by ear here. But just trust me. It'll all work out.

"I do. Trust me. It'll all be fine."

<end memory2458>

<processing memory34790>

<verifying>

<memoryowner toniomanliban confirmed>

\<verification complete>
\<running>

"Please stop coming here, Kuya."

"Anjo, I just need a few hundred thousand bucks to get back on my feet. Please."

"That's what you said last time. And you spent it all on SBX."

"I won't! I just need it to tide me over so I can apply for this new job I'm looking at."

It's true. Though I may also need a little SBX so I can hack my brain to work right just to get through the interview. I'll be a mess without it! I'm a mess right now! Shit, I should have taken a hit before coming here. I have to get Anjo to listen to me. I can't function... my brain can't function right without it. Brains were never meant to run on their own anyway. Our minds were meant to be hacked... to be made better and more powerful. Anjo will see that when I use the SBX to get that job!

"Have you gone to the rehab center like I suggested?"

Oh God, not this again.

"I told you I don't need rehab!"

"So you'd rather I call the cops and you stay in jail instead?"

"Hey, fuck you! You think you're so great because you've got the fancy coding job and the apartment. You were able to get all of that because of me! Because I worked my butt off so you could go to school! Because I stabbed our father with a knife so he wouldn't kill you! I still have the fucking knife, you know. I keep it with me to remind me. And in case he ever comes back. But I still have it."

"Is that a threat?"

"No! I... I'm just saying you owe me, Anjo! You owe me everything and all I'm asking is for some cash!"

"I know I owe you a lot. But I earned that scholarship myself. And I let you stay with me the last two years when I got my first job, I gave you food and a place to stay when you got fired because your boss found out you were mind hacking with SBX. Wasn't that enough to pay you back for what you did for me? But you haven't had a job in months. And you were bringing that crap here into my home. What if the cops found you, found all that SBX here? Do you know what would happen to me at the office? I asked you to stop, to get rid of it, but you never listen."

"I promise, just give me the money, and I'll give it up!"

"I don't believe you. I see it in your eyes. You're going to hack the moment you leave here."

Fuck you!

"Fuck you!"

"Kuya, I can't enable what you're doing to yourself anymore. The only way I'll ever help you is if you go to that rehab center I brought you to before."

You little shit! Don't you dare close that door on me! Don't you dare!

"Don't close that door on me, Anjo! You little shit! Don't you… Anjo! Anjo!!! Open this door!!!"

Dammit! God, I need a hit! I think I have one left at the hostel.

<end memory34790>
<processing memory34850>
<verifying>
<memoryowner toniomanliban confirmed>
<partial corruption>
<patching>
<patching>
<running>

Ungrateful little… Who does he think he is? I'm…

GOD ALMIGHTY I FEEL SO SMALL. I FEEL LIKE A GERM. GERMS CAUSE SICKNESS AND DESTROY. SHOULD I GO AND DESTROY?

Ugh. Something must have gone wrong with that last brain hack. The hunger sensation hasn't been fully shut off. I can still feel it. I…

… IS SOMEONE TRYING TO MAKE ME FEEL HUNGER AGAIN? WHY WOULD ANYONE DO THAT? DO THEY HATE ME?

I only upped the SBX level a little bit compared to last time. If I can just get a bit more, I can do a full hack and shut off all sensation. Then I wouldn't feel anything. If I can't feel anything, I could do anything with no fear. Maybe I could hack my mind into knowing kung fu! Damn, if I had hacked my brain sooner, I wouldn't have needed this knife to fight off Dad. I could have killed him with my bare hands.

I AM ALL-POWERFUL! I HAVE HACKED MYSELF ON THE PATH TO BECOMING A GOD! I WILL BE A VENGEFUL GOD! PITY THOSE WHO WOULD OPPOSE ME!

Oh my God. I can't… my brain is running away from me! I can't control my thoughts anymore. Have I damaged my brain?

I CAN DESTROY THINGS WITH MY MIND!

No! Anjo was right. I need help. I… I want to be better. I have to go to that rehab center. Maybe they can help me. Maybe then Anjo will help me again. I have to go. I need to bring my knife. It's not safe out there.

ISDADCOMINGBACKOHGODNOHEMIGHTCOME BACKIDONTWANTTOUSETHISAGAIN

Where's the address again? Shit, I keep forgetting how to use this stupid Mindseye outside of hacking! I… slyoiuyd??4%67y

<read error>
<bad blocks in memory784575mrdb>
<read error>
<bad blocks in memory784576mrdb >
<read error>
<bad blocks in memory784577mrdb >
<skipping>

Is this the place? It looks right? What time is it?

THISISWRONGMAYBEISHOULDNTBEHERETHEY
MIGHTBECOMINGFORME

This place doesn't look safe. Hold your knife. It will protect you. It has always protected you.

ISDADCOMINGBACKOHGODNOHEMIGHTCOME
BACKIDONTWANTTOUSETHISAGAIN

<read error>
<bad blocks in memory784579mrdb >
<skipping>

It's closed! No! Let me in! Dammit! THEY DON'T WANT ME TO GET IN! WHAT ARE THEY HIDING?

Maybe in the back. Maybe there's still some way to get in the back.

There's a back door. Will they let me in? They have to let me in OR ARE THEY TRYING TO KEEP ME OUT? IS THERE SOMETHING THEY DON'T WANT TO SHOW ME?

Wait. Someone's coming out.

"Hello. C-Can I help you, sir?"

"I-I need help."

"You've come to the right place, if maybe not the best time. But you're lucky I was working a bit late tonight. I was about to head home, but I think I can stay a bit longer to help you. My name's Criselle. What's your name?"

"I-I'm Tonio. Tonio Manliban."

"Hi, Tonio. Why don't you come with me you LITTLE SHIT!"

What?! What the hell?!

"YOU REALLY THOUGHT YOU COULD GET AWAY FROM ME, YOU LITTLE SHIT?"

Dad? How can you be here?! She turned into Dad!

"YOU'RE USELESS. I TOLD YOU YOU WERE USELESS. NOW

I'M GOING TO KILL YOU FOR STABBING ME. SAME WAY I KILLED YOUR MOTHER, YOU LITTLE SHIT!"

No you're not! NO YOU'RE NOT! AARRRRGGHHH!!!

DIE! DIE! DIE! YOU WILL NEVER HURT ME AGAIN, YOU FUCKER! DIE!!!!

"T-Tonio? Wh...Why?"

Oh my God! It's not Dad! It's the girl. What... What did I do?! Oh shit! Oh shit! I'm sorry! I'm so so sorry! I have to run! I have to get out of here! Run!!!

<end memory784585mrdb>

<finishing upload>

<reuploading memoriesconsc of owner jetherbilanan>

<mental integration completed>

The Qualialator gave out a ping. Sgt. Neil removed the helmet from Jether's head.

"Welcome back," Sgt. Neil said as he helped Jether up.

"What did you do to me?" Jether demanded as he slapped Sgt. Neil's hand away from him.

"Sorry, I was planning to talk you into letting Dennis plug you into the machine. I didn't think you'd attack me, you crazy bastard," Sgt. Neil explained as he rubbed his arm.

"So you... set me up?" Jether said in disbelief.

"Sort of," Sgt. Neil shrugged. "The backed up memories of Tonio... You know, the ones they're supposed to put back in his head after he goes through your memories? Dennis found out the machine can also use them for uploading."

"I thought he said memories for upload had to be picked by someone or it couldn't be read?" Jether asked, sounding rather annoyed.

"I... might have lied a bit about that," Dennis sheepishly confessed. "It's what we officially tell people, just so we can get the proper certification and clearances from the government. Mental privacy concerns and what not. But truth be told, I found out the Qualialator was able to pull out usable memories that stood out when it cut and pasted Tonio's full memories and consciousness into its storage. They were involuntarily given, but the Qualialator was able to process them."

"When I found out you volunteered for this pilot program, Jether, I knew what you were really going to do. I told Dennis about it but I didn't know how to stop you. Maybe I could stop you from doing it today, but you'd keep trying to find ways to kill the boy. I knew you wouldn't stop," Sgt. Neil sighed.

"So you thought putting his memories into my mind... would change it? You thought it would make me not want to kill him?" Jether asked.

"I don't know," Sgt. Neil shrugged. "Like I told Dennis when he suggested this plan, it all depends if his tech really works the way it's supposed to."

Dennis gave out a quick nervous laugh before falling silent.

Sgt. Neil slowly walked towards the Qualialator and placed the helmet back on Tonio's head. Then pointed to the LED control screen.

"If you press this button, it will erase Tonio's mind and all his memories stored in the machine." Sgt. Neil moved his finger to another part of the screen. "It will permanently turn him into a vegetable. His body will shut down soon after. All that will be left of his mind will be those memories in your head, Jether."

"What are you..." Jether asked with a puzzled expression on his face.

"Dennis and I are going to quietly leave the room and leave you alone with the boy," Sgt. Neil continued. "If you decide to press the button, we won't tell anybody anything. As far as anyone else will know, this experimental machine malfunctioned and he died in an unfortunate accident."

"And you'd be OK with that?" asked Jether.

"If that machine putting you in Tonio's shoes won't stop you from killing him, then maybe this whole system is bullshit and he won't actually be rehabilitated anyway," Sgt. Neil shrugged. "Then you'd be right and killers won't change."

Sgt. Neil then opened the door to the room. Dennis stepped out first and Sgt. Neil followed. Before closing the door, he gave his friend a warm smile. "But Criselle was trying to help him… to save him. The last thing she ever did was try to save him. You saw that, right? She believed anyone could be saved. And I'm going to bet that she was right."

With that, Sgt. Neil quietly closed the door and left Jether alone with the still unresponsive Tonio.

Jether walked to the console and stared intently at the erase button on it. He stared at it for a good minute or so. Then he looked over to Tonio, whose eyes were slightly twitching. It was a strange experience for Jether. It felt like he was looking at his own face.

Jether then closed his eyes. He had his Mindseye pull up the visualization Criselle had made for him when she was a child. He had always kept a copy of it in all of the Mindseyes he ever had. He mentally zoomed in on it, cropping the drawing of him fighting "bad bugs" out of his mental frame, and focusing on the butterflies and ladybugs cheering him on. He then heard Criselle's voice in his head, even though he knew he had never recorded that particular conversation in his Mindseye. But it sounded so clear, as if she were sitting right beside him.

"And I trust in you. Don't you trust in me?"

EXCHANGES OF FIRE

The mentorship between the student authors and the professional writers was a crucial element of this project, as generations of writers exchange advice, ideas, and emotions about not only the craft but about the issue of extrajudical killings.

Here is a glimpse into some of the mentoring that guided the works in this book.

JAN ONG ON BEING MENTORED BY EXIE ABOLA FOR HER STORY "BAPTISM BY FIRE"

When I first heard we were going to have mentors, my initial thought was, "Yay, someone's going to check my grammar!" But it really evolved. In the beginning I was also kind of intimidated as well because I knew that mentorship would mean that this person is really going to be criticizing... well, not really criticizing your work but will be trying to help you improve it. There's something a little scary about that. But I was really excited.

When I met with my mentor Exie, I had batchmates who were actually his students for merit English and Literature. They were all telling me, "Oh no! Exie really checks grammar! He's so hard to please!" I was like, "Oh no! I'm so scared!" But when I actually met with him... I remember it was during the Christmas break and there was no school... when he was giving me his comments I thought, "Oh my gosh! These comments are so helpful!" I would have never thought of them. I really appreciated that he didn't actually focus on grammar and descriptions. It was really about the development of my character and how I could improve it. And the stuff he was saying really made so much sense. I was really, really happy that I was open to it and that he really gave me those value-adding comments. I really feel like my story wouldn't have been as good if he wasn't able to help me extract those things. What was really nice was that he didn't just give me the answers but he helped me figure them out on my own.

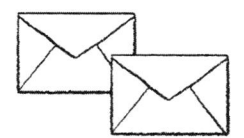

After Patricia Narvasa ("Control") was paired with Christine V. Lao ("What Damage") as her mentor, Pat found out that coincidentally Tin was a family friend. The following are letters Pat and Tin sent to each other during the mentorship process.

Dear Ma'am Tin,

I cannot say that I wrote the first draft of "Control" with the best intentions. The story was a requirement during my freshman year, and I wrote it to comply. I began by bouncing off my ideas with my friends during our breaks and by researching stories about EJK child victims. I had an idea of how I wanted to write the story but struggled to write it. Like any other student, I procrastinated writing the story until the night before it was due. I have always done better when under pressure, so I hoped with all the planning, I would be able to give the stories of these victims some justice.

When Ma'am Martin assigned the work, Kian Delos Santos had just been killed. We all knew what had happened, but we were also in a bubble away from it. It was easy to forget about it after a while. It was easier to forget about the other children that had been killed before and after Kian.

When I began my research on EJK child victims, I barely found any reporting on EJK cases. There was not much information then. The story I got inspiration from was the story of five-year-old Danica Mae Garcia and her family. Danica Mae, in her pink graduation robe, is still stuck in my head whenever I think about EJK. Her family complied with the government. Her grandfather was in a list of suspected drug pushers and upon hearing of this, he surrendered willingly to clear his name. Yet they were still targeted, and Danica Mae still 'had' to die for the sake of this war.

It is hard to think about all the children dying for no reason. There are so many kids younger than I am who are getting killed, and their deaths are

*just considered a necessary evil. When I wrote the first draft of "Control,"
I had just started college. I had so many plans for my future. I chose to
write about Danica Mae because she was her family's favorite, she was
an obedient, happy, and all-around good child. She just graduated from
preschool. Her whole life was ahead of her; but then her life was cut.
Did anyone even care about her plans and her future? Danica Mae had
become a casualty, someone whom we would soon forget.*

*At first, I went off on the cliché that the youth is the future, that the
loss of a child is the loss of the potential greatness that a child could
have brought to the world. But as I worked on my draft, I began asking
myself how true these statements were. I eventually concluded that if
they were true, we wouldn't love rags to riches stories as much as we
do. We love these stories because of their rarity. It allows us to believe
we can overcome anything, but often hard work is not enough to get a
success story.*

*I study at Ateneo, one of the most prestigious and expensive schools in the
Philippines. Most members of my family studied there too. I always knew
that I would go to college and be able to work towards anything I want
to do, but would Danica Mae have been given the same opportunities
that I have? The prevalence of poverty and the struggle that the poor are
facing to meet their daily needs hinder many of them from getting the
proper resources to have the same opportunities. It seemed more likely
to me that they would remain in poverty, because of how broken our
systems are.*

*I wanted my story to show how some people do not just use drugs for the
sake of it. Some people believe it is the only solution. They use it to escape
from the trauma they have experienced. Some turn to selling drugs to*

support their families because that is the only way they know how to make money. I wanted to show how the Drug War and EJK are not the solutions to our country's problems. As long as our government does not address the root of poverty, these drug users/pushers, people living in poverty will continue to become victims of extrajudicial killings, will continue to be the scapegoat to our country's problems.

I think your work highlights something important in how some people see EJK victims. They see their deaths as a necessary evil to eradicate the drug problem. Danica Mae is just collateral damage; she is just another statistic, another child lost in the cracks of our broken society. It shows how the government fails the people who need them the most. It also suggests that these deaths are held up as proof that the government is doing something. They are trying to give people a false sense of security: one less user/pusher on the streets is thought to make the country safer. But are we actually safer? How are we safer when children are being killed without any justice?

I always knew that I am privileged, that I was given all the tools that ensure I will succeed and be sheltered from many horrors. I probably live a life opposite to the reality of Danica Mae. Knowing this, I have always been taught that I should use my privilege to help amplify the voices that are being silenced. This is what attracted me to this project, but it also made me question if I had the right to tell a story I didn't experience. I am an Atenean who probably has the smallest idea of what is really happening on the streets. However, one thing I've always loved about literature is that it allows someone to tell a story that is far from their reality. Literature holds the truth about life, even when it is fiction. In my succeeding drafts, I moved away from facts specific to Danica Mae because I did not want to misrepresent anyone's story. Having done so,

I find that the final version of "Control" represents the story of many others.

I wrote this story when I was 18, only a year older than Kian. Although I didn't think I would be able to properly portray the systemic injustices that caused both Kian's and Danica Mae's deaths, I wrote "Control" anyway, hoping that my story would be able to shed a little bit of light on the reality of the Philippines.

I think an important part of this project is that we are trying to give a voice to this issue. Although the stories may be fictional, we are trying to present different perspectives, giving voice to people who believe they have none. With everything that has been happening recently with the government trying to silence its critics, when else are we supposed to use our voices but now? All my life, everyone has taught me to appreciate the freedom of speech that my grandparents and parents fought for. We often overlook this freedom because we forget what their generations had to go through for us to have it, so what right do I have now to stay silent when our country is being threatened again?

Sincerely,
Patricia

Dear Pat,

When Cyan asked if I'd like to mentor a college student who had written a story in response to the Duterte Government's War on Drugs, I was astonished. I myself found it difficult to write in response to the unthinkable—a government killing its own people. I could not find the words. Perhaps there was something this young student could teach me. In exchange, I would offer what little I knew about making short stories.

I was impressed by the audacity of your first draft of "Control." It described how the narrator, a child victim of Tokhang, wakes up and finds that her body has survived, but she is no longer in control of it. I likewise admired the fact that you had based your draft on careful research: you had included details surrounding the case of five-year-old Danica Mae Garcia of Dagupan City, who was killed during a Tokhang operation. "Collateral damage," our government officials called her.

The project editors commented that your draft ended just when the real story began. You needed to imagine what would happen if the narrator had to witness her body grow up —go to school, fall in love—as she watched helplessly. And so we sat together one day, outlining the imagined life of a disembodied narrator, scene by scene.

While other writers, myself included, would have been paralyzed at the outset by questions of representation—Do I know enough of Danica Mae to imagine her as a teenager? Who am I to speak for Drug War victims?— you managed to sidestep the issue by moving away from Danica Mae's story. You began a new draft that felt closer to your own experiences and what you know about life. You invented a new character, built a world around her, completely imagined, yet still familiar. Imagination provided the path to think the unthinkable—the future that Danica Mae, and other child victims of Tokhang, never had.

After reading "Control," I came away with the following insight: Tokhang's victims include not just the thousands killed; each one of us who survives it—drug user or no— is a victim too. Tokhang's unreasoned relentlessness might make it seem that survival is all; so we turn against each other, our lust for control underscoring how powerless we actually feel. Our much-touted resilience in the face of systematic state-sponsored violence masks how broken we are as individuals, and as a people.

I admit that your ending made me pause and think: does the narrator take too much responsibility for what happens in the end? This is why I wrote "What Damage," which, I hope, reminds us of others who ought to take responsibility, but do not.

"What Damage" operates as a collage. Dictionary definitions of the word "collateral" are jumbled with words and phrases cut out from news articles and reports on the Government's War on Drugs. Those who use the term "collateral damage" render each child victim into a mere statistic, an afterthought. Those who use it to refer to Danica Mae are the same people who most need to read your story. If only they thought as carefully as you did. If only they imagined as deeply.

With admiration,
Tin

Jamie Bautista ("The Life Penalty") and Katarina
Rodriguez ("Self-Proclaimed Hero") reflect on the
creative journey they went on mentoring each other
for this anthology over the course of three years.

KAT RECALLS WRITING HER SHORT STORY

In my first year of college, I was taking this lit class with Ma'am Joyce. We had this final requirement where we could either submit an analysis of a story about extrajudicial killings in the Philippines or we could write our own stories. Initially, I wanted to do the analysis of the given story because I was really concerned about the issue. I also felt it was so much work to write a short story since I normally like to write poetry and not stories. But when I read the story and I honestly got really confused. I was like, "There's no way I can do an analysis on this!" And the assignment was due in a couple of days so I thought, "Crap! I need to do something!" I was so scared! I did my story in one sitting because I was really anxious about it. I just said to myself, "Screw it! I'll just submit it. I'm OK if I just get a C or C+. I just want to pass!"

I asked my classmates, "What did you guys do?" And they were like, "Oh, we wrote the short stories. Seemed easy enough." Then I asked, "How long were your stories?" And they said, "Mine's fifteen pages," and another said, "Mine's twenty." And I thought, "Oh god! I'm so screwed!"

A couple of days later, Ma'am Joyce talked to the whole class, "There are two people that I would like to talk to after this class. It's regarding the short stories you submitted. The two people I want to talk to are Pat Narvasa and Kat..." There was another Kat in our class, so I thought it was her, but then she goes, "...Rodriguez." And I thought, "Oh god! She's going to get mad at my shitty work! I failed the class! She's going to kill me!" I was so scared that when I approached I was shaking! I was about to apologize, but then she said, "I really liked your stories." Oh my god! She's congratulating me! And then she started talking about the publishing thing and I started to freak out. What the hell? I wrote this paper in one sitting! What is happening?

I got so excited! I literally called my mom right after and she got really excited for me too. Then she kinda got a little scared for me when I told her what the topic of the story was, but she was still really excited for me. So that's how I got into this whole thing. And I was really proud that I did work like that because it was about something I was passionate about but worried about at the same time because I had never really written short stories before. I was expecting to fail then the extreme opposite happened.

JAMIE EXPLAINS HOW HE JOINED THE PROJECT

I remember getting an email from Cyan Abad-Jugo back in March of 2018 to join this project which would eventually become *Triggered*. She mentioned that she and Joyce Martin were working on an anthology collecting young adult fiction stories by students in Joyce's class. They had discussed the project with Karina Bolasco of Ateneo Press, who suggested that they bring in professional authors to mentor the students in getting their works ready for publication, especially since these students were not literature majors. While I found the project interesting and the subject matter relevant and important, I was initially planning to decline her invitation. Living in Alabang, the thought of having to brave hours of traffic driving all the way to Ateneo in Quezon City just to mentor a student seemed like too much of a hassle. Also, I was at a point in my life where I didn't want to be involved in anything remotely political. Being the nephew of Noynoy Aquino and grand-nephew of Cory Aquino meant that political discussions always got too personal and stressful. After the 2016 election cycle, I had been avoiding political issues for my own mental health, despite hating the rising culture of violence being promoted by the new administration that was causing deaths all over the country. But for some reason, I hadn't answered Cyan's email yet, maybe because I hadn't figured out how to politely decline.

That same week I received the email, I was invited by my actor friend Teetin Villanueva to watch a play she was performing in. It was Dulaang UP's production of "The Kundiman Party", written by Floy Quintos and directed by Dexter Santos. The play is about a retired Kundiman singer named Maestra Adela, her student Antoinette (played by Teetin), Antoinette's activist boyfriend Bobby, and the Maestra's three friends who create a viral online video series that melds discussions of the fine arts and nationalism with kundiman performances dubbed "The Kundiman Party". When Bobby insists that videos also talk about EJK when the brother of Adela's household help is killed, the group is targeted by pro-government forces. At a planned culminating activity for the Kundiman Party, Bobby's estranged father, who is part of the administration, tells him that playing with the arts is just a pastime that will have no effect, challenging him to join armed rebels if he seriously wants to fight back. Bobby leaves the Kundiman Party, his final decision unknown, breaking Antoinette's heart. Still, Antoinette goes on to sing kundiman for supporters who arrive and they push through with the event.

At the end of the play, I found myself sympathizing with Antoinette. Perhaps I was more focused on Antoinette as a character simply because Teetin played her so well and made her conflict and journey so relatable (and I remember she mentioned Sir Floy may have based some aspects of the character on her). But what Antoinette did in the final scene really struck me. Despite all the threats that caused their group to believe protesting against EJK was either too dangerous or pointless, Antoinette decided to continue singing because she saw that it would inspire others. I felt she realized that people like Bobby want to fight fire with fire and end up becoming just like the people they despise. They would abandon the arts and the welfare of others if these hindered or didn't serve their own goals. But Adela described kundiman to Antoinette as a means of singing that attracts people with an unusually strong emotional pull that is almost impossible to resist. It was what Antoinette used to get Bobby to commit to her at the start of the play. At the end, even when he was gone, Antoinette decided to continue using it to draw others in, however slowly, to their cause. I felt that her tearfully singing that last kundiman song was her making a brave statement about how she would go on and not give up. As the cast made their curtain call, it hit me that I wanted to be like Antoinette and similarly use art to attract people towards a culture that valued life and dignity. Even if I didn't want to overtly protest against those using violence, I could help create an artistic culture that would naturally reject violence and those who benefit from it. This may be more my interpretation of the story, as Sir Floy has since told me he was pleasantly surprised by my take on the ending, but it's the reading of the play I came to internalize.

While there is need for people to fight or protest (especially for those who are not politically pigeonholed like me), I felt that my special role as an artist was not to be against something, but to be for something. I had to use my art to attract people to the values that were the polar opposite of the things I felt were wrong in our country. Like kundiman, I had to pull people towards something good, rather than just pushing away those who promoted evil. The day after seeing the play was when I read Cyan's email to me again. And that's when I realized that this project could be the perfect chance to practice this newfound philosophy. This was a project that was against the issue of EJK, similar to the video series in "The Kundiman Party". Could I use this as an opportunity to inspire a young person to use their literary talent to not just be against EJK but to promote a culture of art, empathy and love that would then organically displace one of pragmatic violence? Could I do what I imagined in my own head canon what Antoinette was doing after the events of the play? Besides, I thought to myself that if I had been willing to drive out to Quezon City to watch a play (twice, as I would watch "The Kundiman Party" the week after), how could I complain about braving traffic a few times a month to go to Ateneo for this project?

So I emailed Cyan back. I told her to count me in.

KAT ON THE MENTORSHIP ASPECT OF THE PROJECT

I was actually a little worried initially because I was afraid my story was going to change so drastically in a way that I didn't want it to go. I was really worried that Jamie was going to be strict with the little details and really nitpick everything. But after our first meeting and several meetings after, I felt comfortable with editing my story and having him double check everything. I felt it was like he had the best interests of my story in mind and he knew what he was doing more than I was. And he was leading my story in a direction that I actually wanted it to go. My story started out a lot different from what it is now and I really like the changes that happened. His perspectives on my story brought out the best in it, and I think that happened a lot when we were meeting. I think we communicated very well.

It also didn't feel so tiresome or exhausting meeting to edit because he and I would talk and we'd joke around and it would be really funny and light when we would edit my story. So I really liked the process as I got into it. And I also like that he let me read his story and let me have inputs also in it. So I felt there was a really good dynamic where we were comfortable enough and we trusted each other enough to work on each other's stories. And it was a very easy process.

JAMIE ON THEIR PEER MENTORING PROCESS

Unlike many of the other mentors on this project, I was not actively teaching at any university when I came on board. It had been eleven years since I had last taught, despite having taught writing and art classes part-time at various schools over the years. I had stopped teaching in 2007 when I decided to take my masters in Entrepreneurship, feeling that it was time for me to take on the role of a student again. And in the years since I told myself I didn't want to check papers or plan lectures and submit grades again, despite being asked several times in those years to teach at Ateneo. But this mentoring project felt like a good middle ground where it was just a few sessions working with a single student and for a limited time only (or so I thought).

I met Kat during our initial orientation session in Areté on May 21, 2018. I had already read Kat's story via email a few days prior. I remember Cyan telling me that we were paired up because Kat's story was short and action-packed, and as a graphic novel writer Cyan felt my sensibilities were the best fit. After Kat and I were introduced we went to one side of the room to talk. Kat told me how she hadn't really written a story before and she actually didn't enjoy writing stores since it made her feel anxious from self-doubt. I told Kat that part of our goal would be to have her enjoy writing so that hopefully she would continue to create more stories in the future.

Our first few interactions for the mentorship were done via email, as I had warned Kat that I may not be able to go to Ateneo that often. I sent Kat an essay I used to share with my English students in Ateneo back in 2003 entitled "Shitty First Drafts" which was meant to ease her worries about writing since even experienced writers like me still feel imposter syndrome when we write that first terrible written-in-white-heat draft. I also shared with her a copy of my comic *Private Iris* which was written in a first-person perspective and from the point-of-view of the criminal, very similar to Kat's story.

I had also made some suggestions regarding her story. The first draft was quite different from the final published version. It was really short, just a page or so and could be considered flash fiction. Initially, the protagonist was a man who worked alone. The story was written in the past tense, which was typical for most prose stories. And the story originally ended simply with the assassin, after killing the child of his target, asking the cops who hired him for his payment. I asked Kat to think about possible plot holes in the story, such as why the police would pay a killer who did not actually kill their intended target. I mentioned that many extrajudicial killings were done by tandems and she may want to consider giving her protagonist a partner, which would also allow give him someone to converse with in the story. But the biggest tip I gave was for her to focus her theme. What was the story trying to say, aside from "EJK is bad"? In my email, I wrote, "The way I see your story is that it's supposed to make a value judgement on the beliefs of your protagonist (that they're wrong or misguided). I think I mentioned this to you during our talk, but I wanted to bring up again the possible approaches you can have towards your theme."

Because part of the project was for me to also write a response piece to Kat's story, I told Kat that I wanted her input in crafting my own story. I told her that because I technically wasn't a teacher, I didn't want her to see me as someone teaching her how to write. Instead, I wanted the two of us to see each other as peer mentors who were sharing writing processes with each other. Kat got a glimpse of how structured I am as a writer when I gave her a list of five story ideas I had come up with as a response to her piece. I asked her to choose which one I would develop into a full story. I wanted her to be very involved in my writing process and to have a hand in the story as well. Of the five ideas I gave her, I was silently hoping she wouldn't pick the one sci-fi concept I had because I knew it would be the most difficult to write and would result in a long story as I would have to do a lot of world-building. Of course, Kat chose the sci-fi story.

Weeks later, after Kat had done some revisions and I had just started plotting out my story, we agreed to meet up at Ateneo for some face-to-face mentoring sessions. Since I wasn't a faculty member and did not have a desk or office in the campus, we were really lucky that our project was considered an Areté Sandbox residency, which provided us access to a study room in the building. That study room became our regular meeting place for our mentoring sessions over the next few weeks.

We truly got to see how different our creative processes were. Kat liked free flow writing, where she would just write on the page not quite knowing where the story would go. I showed her my Excel file that had all my scenes plotted out and my ten-page outline detailing the laws, rules, and future tech of my sci-fi world. And yet I had only written maybe two pages at that time. I would bounce ideas off of her and get her feedback if she thought some of the technobabble or concepts I created were clear and not incomprehensible. She would ask me if her story's theme was starting to form and have more focus.

One of the biggest changes Kat made to her story was to have her protagonist be a woman, specifically a mother. I liked that idea as it gave Kat more layers of the character to explore. It also provided a more sympathetic reason for the character to accept the horrible task of killing someone. After all, one theme that both Kat and I decided to have in our stories was to look at the issue of EJK from the perspective of someone on the other side of the political fence. Kat didn't want to just judge her character for being wrong. She wanted readers to understand why such a person would ever think killing was acceptable. The fact that her protagonist was doing it for her own children added humanity to the character. I felt it could open up genuine discussions about why people would ever think violence is an answer. We did also have to adjust the ending and show character's actions backfiring. Kat did want to show that violence may seem like a necessary solution, but contributing to that culture will come back to haunt you. We had a lot of discussions about the repercussions might be, what role the police and her partner would be, and so on. In the end, we felt the piece ended up being tighter thematically.

My story was truly inspired by Kat's. Because her story was about entering the mind of a killer, I came up with the idea of having a future where killers would be punished by forcing them to live through their victims' memories. My story's theme was also similar to Kat's: that we need to understand others in order to make meaningful change. So my story also had to have my protagonist, who would be pro-EJK like Kat's protagonist, enter the mind of the drug-user who killed his child. The story had to have him, and the readers, learn what would push a person to take drugs and commit crimes. I told Kat that setting my story in the future might help readers separate themselves from the politics of the issue and focus on the actual values and ethics behind it. Kat and I brainstormed about how far in the future it would be set, what kind of tech would exist in that time, and how even drugs would change, even if the overall motivation for taking them may still be the same. These conversations would then lead into us talking about how different our generations are. I would ask her about trends I didn't understand while sharing "In my day…" type memories of Ateneo. And yet there were many things and values we still had in common.

We both decided to play around with tenses and point-of-view to help make our stories more immersive. I had suggested to Kat that she write her story in the present tense, similar to how movie scripts were written, to make the action seem more urgent and to add to the suspense. I also challenged her to maintain her story's first-person perspective, so only her character's inner narration could describe actions and setting. She had to make it all feel like a person's natural thoughts and not sound like exposition. For my story, I would have a third-person omniscient narrator speaking in the past tense for scenes happening in the real world the switch to a first-person perspective narrated in the present tense (similar to Kat's story) for scenes happening in the virtual world. So our stories not only had thematic similarities but stylistic ones as well.

In August of 2018, as part of our Areté Sandbox residency our group got to attend the Improv-ing Empathy acting workshop with Missy Maramara. As a theater geek, I was excited to about attending this. Kat mentioned she would be joining as well. But when the day arrived, Kat wasn't there and we received the shocking news that her father had suddenly passed away due to a health issue. I quickly texted Kat my condolences, not really knowing what else to say. We met up a few weeks later for a writing session at Areté and I honestly wasn't sure how to ask how she was doing. But by then she seemed to have already accepted what had happened and shared with me the difficult story of how she found out her dad had died. In a later session, I had to write a scene where my character had to identify his daughter's body in the morgue. Kat generously shared with me the emotions she went through in processing her dad's sudden passing, and she helped me write about a type of grief I could barely even imagine. I was really grateful that Kat trusted me enough to share with me what her grieving process was. That was truly one way Kat taught me how to empathize when writing.

By late 2018, we were mostly communicating via email every once in a while as Kat's story was mostly done and I was busy working on another personal project. Cyan had given us a deadline of December 30 to submit our final drafts. Kat had submitted her story a few days early. The day before the deadline I was still several pages away from completing the story, so I locked myself in my empty office (my staff was already on holiday leave) and wrote like a madman for a few hours until I finally finished it. We had both submitted our stories and all we had to do now was wait for the book to get published. But come 2019, the updates on the project started to dwindle. By the middle of the year, there was no news on the progress of the book. Kat and I also lost touch by then, since we assumed the mentoring phase of the project was done. By the end of that year, I was starting to think that the book might not actually get published. But at the very least, I was glad to have had the experience peer mentoring with Kat as we crafted our stories.

KAT ON THE PAUSE OF THE PROJECT IN 2019

Through that one year in 2019 where we didn't touch our stories, my studies really strengthened my advocacy. It made my feelings about my story stronger because I did a lot of research papers during the time we didn't touch our stories. I was able to read more on the topic of EJK in my Political Science classes. For my Theology class, I had to sit in a room where people were talking about their actual experiences with EJK, like when their child was killed and everything. So it didn't really change my story but it strengthened it because I had a better perspective. And it gave me this drive to work on the project a lot more and really focus my attention to that project. So I went back and reread my story and compared it to the things I researched. I just wanted to make sure that everything was right so that when we got back to editing my story in 2020, I could add the necessary pieces to make it better. I felt everything was just intensified. I had this new drive to keep working on it and hopefully make a bit of difference with the story that I've written.

JAMIE RECALLS THEIR NEW MENTORSHIP PROCESS IN 2020

2020 of course was not only the start of a new decade, it was also the beginning of a global pandemic that would change all our lives and all the plans we had imagined for ourselves the year before. In the middle of 2019, Martin Villanueva, who was then chairperson of the Ateneo Fine Arts Department and who had given our project its Areté Sandbox residency, had invited me to teach. Because of the great experience I had mentoring for the anthology (and because I had already gotten used to braving traffic to go to the Ateneo) I agreed. My first semester teaching started in January of 2020, but it was cut short in March due to the sudden arrival of the quarantines caused by COVID-19. I didn't get to finish the semester with my first batch of students, and yet I still continued teaching in the semesters that followed using Zoom and learning management systems to teach online. Strangely, because teaching was now online, I was actually able to take on more classes as distance and traffic were no longer factors. I had been given a new opportunity to share with even more young people the lessons I had learned from "The Kundiman Party": how to use their art to promote a culture of empathy that would also displace violence and authoritarianism as the path to our country's prosperity.

While the pandemic had put a lot of other plans on hold, it had strangely become the time when our EJK anthology project suddenly came back to life. Cyan and Joyce emailed me to update me on the progress of the book. Apparently, their original publisher would not be able to add the book to their publishing lineup in the near future due to the backlog caused by the pandemic. Both Joyce and Cyan wanted the book though to be done by the time our student writers graduated in 2021. That was when I offered to publish the book under my own small publishing company. Suddenly, our project was up and running again. Cyan set new deadlines allowing all the writers to take another look at their stories and update or revise them if necessary. I got back in touch with Kat and asked her if she wanted to us to revisit our stories and do new edits given the space and distance of a year from our last drafts. She agreed and over the course of the next few months, we would meet up via Skype and Zoom for a session between each new semester (as that was when we both were not busy). Though we hadn't talked in over a year, it felt like no time had passed and we had picked up right where we had left off. I would ask her advice about how to best teach students like her over Canvas and Google Meet, she would rant about classes, and we would refine our stories further, discussing some of the new comments Cyan had on our last drafts.

During one session, I remember that Kat had mentioned having a hard time planning out the action in her story because it was difficult to picture the setting of her story. So I screen-shared Photoshop from my laptop during a Skype call and I sketched out a map of the setting of her story, asking her

questions about locations and where characters would be positioned, all to help clarify the logistics of the story in her head. It was a fun exercise that showed that even distance and a pandemic could not stop our mentorship.

Also during 2020, an old friend of mine from high school got in touch with me to help their friend who had been arrested on drug charges. I ended up calling contacts who had experience working with shelters and recovering addicts for legal advice. The things I learned from helping my friend opened my eyes to the reality of what drug users were going through. It not only helped me flesh out the details of the drug user in my story more during my new round of editing, it also allowed me to share with Kat a deeper and clearer perspective on the issue of the drug problem in the country.

We would continue to have virtual meet-ups every few months until mid-2021, right as the book, now with the title *Triggered*, was being finalized. By this time, Kat was no longer the incoming college sophomore who was scared of writing stories I had met three years ago. She was now a law student, telling me about the tons of cases her professors were making her read and how she was gaining an interest in family law. Given the change in her story to feature a mother willing to kill for her children's sake, I could see why this was the case. I was also no longer just a writer doing this mentorship as a way to remember what it was like being a teacher. I was now back to being a true teacher again with a newfound purpose. It had been over three years and we had changed a lot, but the ease and effectiveness of our peer mentorship was one thing that stayed constant between us over these years.

KAT REFLECTS ON WHAT'S NEXT

I'm going to law school now and the law has always been my advocacy. The reason I wanted to go to law school was because of everything that was happening in the Philippines. I wanted to make a difference in whatever way that I could. Law seemed like the right path for me. I'm learning from everything that we went through and from each of our stories... not just mine and Jamie's but from everyone else's in our project. I realize that you don't stop at where you are when you're fighting for something. You have to keep going and you have to keep thinking far into the future as well on what you can do. That's also why I've directed my career in making a difference in that way. And I feel like all the lessons that I've learned here and this drive and intensity that I've found working in this setting where we really focus on the EJKs, I don't think I'll ever forget about what's happening. These things constantly happen and there's always something that I can do about it. There's always something that I can contribute whether that's going to law school or writing about EJK. I don't have to go out and just protest. There are many different ways that I can contribute to this issue and I really did learn that working on this project. Even if I couldn't go out and protest, I could always write and still make a huge difference in my own way. I'm still speaking out about it and acknowledging that EJK is still happening out there and it needs to be addressed. And I really like that this project highlighted that for me. It didn't even feel like it was three years of working on the stories. It felt really natural and fun. That's why I really enjoyed the project and I'm sad that it's come to an end.

JAMIE ON THE WHAT THE PROJECT MEANS TO HIM

I look back at who I was before this project started. I was someone who didn't want to be involved in anything political out of a fear of conflict. I was blocking people who had different political views. I was withdrawing from things due to fear. I had lost my passion for writing and creating art. I was too lazy to go back to teaching. Now I'm back to teaching several classes each semester, trying to inspire young artists to create art that promotes empathy and brings them prosperity. I'm creating stories that are tackling hot-button, political issues by trying to reach across the aisle to those who have different beliefs. I'm taking risks and reaching out and connecting to more people. I'm still amazed by how much this experience has changed me.

I can't emphasize enough how big of an impact this project has had on my life. It's hard for me not to think there's some grand plan or a purpose behind me becoming involved with this project. There are just too many coincidences. For instance, Missy Maramara facilitated our empathy improv workshop and was also in "The Kundiman Party". That day of the workshop was also when I watched the play "Desaparesidos" (with Teetin cast in this play also) which was directed by Guelan Luarca, who would later be part of the Areté panel discussion group that covered our project. Martin Villanueva used to work at my design studio when he was a fresh graduate and his involvement in the project via Areté would lead him to bring me back to teaching. The themes I wanted to share with my one mentee from our anthology project, I could now share with numerous students over several classes and semesters. And for one of those semesters, Floy Quintos, the playwright behind "The Kundiman Party", gave guest lectures for my Ateneo classes after I told him that his play inspired me to return to teaching. Are these are all just coincidences, or are these more like threads that bound seemingly random events together into a unique story with a powerful message to share?

I sometimes imagine what became of the character of Antoinette from "The Kundiman Party" after the events of the play. My head canon is that she continued to use her singing of kundiman online to inspire others to care about the country. I imagine she blended her sense of business (as she was a management trainee at a big company taking singing lessons on the side) with her art to find a way to expand her online performances into a whole movement that caused others to create their own types of content, all with the similar theme of promoting a Filipino culture of empathy and dignity. I picture her gloating to Bobby that he was wrong to believe his dad that dabbling in art was just a "pastime" that wouldn't make a difference. And I feel inspired that this is something I could actually do myself in real life as well. I look at our little book anthology and see how much it has expanded and grown. I look at how watching a single play has branched out into so many opportunities for me to use my art for good and to inspire others. I see my students who have graduated and who are starting to make their mark in the world. I see my kids as they learn to hone their own artistic skills. I see my theater friends continuing to create inspiring art despite the challenges of the pandemic. I see Kat as she learns to change the world now using knowledge of the law. And I feel hopeful about the future of our country.

I was not triggered by anger or despair. I was positively triggered to act by art, by a play, by stories. And I will always be grateful that I was given this opportunity to trigger the spark of creativity and empathy in others. It's why I hope this book is not the end of a project but rather the beginning of something that will grow, expand, and inspire more young people like Kat and our other student writers to respond to a growing culture of destruction by creating art and spreading a culture of love, empathy, and human dignity.

A CONTINUING RESPONSE

Do you have your own response to our stories and writings? Do you have a response to the issue of extrajudicial killings in the Philippines? Use the extra page here to jot down your thoughts, sketch some artwork, or write your own story or essay. Let your own personal artisic response be a part of your copy of this project. This is a conversation that should continue.

If you wish to share your response with us, we would love to see it! You can email us at triggeredresponse@chambershell.com or submit it to our website at www.chambershell.com/triggered.

MEET THE AUTHORS AND ILLUSTRATORS

The Editors

Cyan Abad-Jugo teaches English and Great Books at the Ateneo de Manila University. Her books include: *Father and Daughter* (with Gémino Abad), *Sweet Summer and Other Stories, Leaf and Shadow: Stories About Some Friendly Creatures,* and *Salingkit: A 1986 Diary.* She has also edited an anthology of short stories for young adults called *Friend Zones* and written four chapter books for children: *Yaya Maya and the White King, The Earth-Healers, Letters From Crispin,* and *The Looking-Glass Tree.* She lives with her husband, hobbits, and wonder cats in QC.

Jocelyn Martin is Assistant Professor in the Department of English of the Ateneo de Manila University, where she is also Managing Editor of *Kritika Kultura.* Holder of a PhD in languages and literatures from the Université Libre de Bruxelles, and member of the Advisory Board of the Memory Studies Association, she researches on memory, trauma, listening, translation, and the environmental humanities. Her forthcoming publications are included in *Bloomsbury History, Theory and Method,* and in the *Handbook of Translation and Memory* (Routledge).

The Authors

Samantha Chiu loves stories. She has lived countless lives, travelled the world, taken on all kinds of jobs, and met numerous inspiring people through different worlds that authors have allowed her to experience and through those she made up herself. Her life is made up of stories and she has a lot of stories to share too. After graduating BS Management Engineering Cum Laude from Ateneo de Manila University, she is currently enjoying the new chapter of her life as she faces adulthood. "Patintero" is a story of hope––pun intended–– spanning the past, present, and what may be. Sam wrote the short story with a goal to symbolize the harsh reality of hope during EJK. Nonetheless, for as long as humans live, hope shall too. Four years ago, teenage Sam hoped to share a story to others one day and here she is now. She now hopes to inspire other people, who have the same dream as her, to share their voices and stories to others. Dreams do come true. When not living through stories of ink, Sam enjoys singing––though not talented, binging all kinds of things, taking on adventures––in thought and through action, spending time with people and attempting to create meaningful impact for everyone she meets.

Amiel Deuna is a BS Management Engineering graduate from the Ateneo de Manila University. His interest in writing started in school publications when he was in grade school and high school. However, "Into the Night" is his first attempt in creating a fictional piece, making this publication a very memorable one for him. The narrative is a realistic fiction piece that emphasizes those who are most affected by these raids: the loved ones of the alleged drug suspects, particularly the children. By seeing these events through the perspective of these children, we can see an irreversible effect that will haunt them for the rest of their lives, and that the world will never be the same for them. Outside of this short story, Amiel enjoys watching movies, cooking and eating food, and discovering new music. He also loves to travel, and he wishes to experience the wonders that the world has to offer.

Red Nadela is the author of "September 28". When he isn't writing, Red works full-time at a financial-technology firm looking to improve the lives of Filipinos day-in and day-out through financial inclusion. Of course, Red has his own assortment of guilty past times, in the forms of gaming, dogsitting, trading, and more. He's especially avid as a Valorant and DotA player in his free time, looking to beat his opponents in the competitive scene and be merciless in doing so. He's fun-loving with his two dogs, Belle (short for Barbell) and Minnie, taking them for daily walks even if he has to wake up early to do so. And when there's more time, he likes going into stocks as his own weird way of passing the time. Cool guy, right? Get close to Red and maybe even get to work with him:
LinkedIn: https://www.linkedin.com/in/ron-edward-nadela/
Email: ron.edward.nadela@gmail.com

Patricia Bianca Tutaan Narvasa, the author of "Control", recently graduated from Ateneo de Manila University with a degree in Bachelor of Arts in Philosophy. Patricia has always had a love for stories. She particularly finds it fascinating to hear about the background behind these narratives. She believes that every great story reflects some form of truth and reality of the storyteller. Growing up in a tight-knit family, Patricia heard many interesting stories from them, particularly those of her grandfathers and their time serving the country as eminent jurists. These men have left a great and lasting legacy behind, as they did better than their best to pursue the truth, fight for justice, and uphold the rule of law. These stories serve as her inspiration and use these as motivation in everything she does.

Jan Ong is the author of "Baptism by Fire". She received her bachelor of science in Management Engineering from the Ateneo de Manila University. More than writing, she loves telling stories in different forms—in everyday conversations, experiences, and even art. When she's not working on another passion project, you might catch her enjoying a good exercise or trying something new!

Katarina Rodriguez is a graduate of the Ateneo de Manila University. She majored in AB Diplomacy and International Relations with a minor degree in Philosophy. She is currently a student in her first year in the Ateneo Law School. Ever since she can remember, Kat has always been passionate about writing and politics. Her first published piece in this anthology reflects the intersection of both her most valued passions. When Kat isn't busying herself with academics, she's cooking or baking, or watching old films, animé, and cartoons.

Exie Abola is a prizewinning writer of stories and essays. His first book, a collection of essays titled *Trafficking in Nostalgia: Essays from Memory*, was published in 2012. His work has been published in literary journals, magazines, and anthologies. He obtained his AB from Ateneo de Manila (Literature: English) and master's degree in Creative Writing from the University of the Philippines–Diliman. He teaches with the Department of English and Fine Arts Program of Ateneo de Manila University as assistant professor. Formerly a lifestyle writer for the *Philippine Star*, he contributes occasionally to the theater section of *The Philippine Daily Inquirer*. He is at work on his first collection of short stories.

Jamie Bautista graduated cum laude from the Ateneo de Manila University with a degree in Communications, and has a Masters in Entrepreneurship degree from the Asian Center for Entrepreneurship and Asian Institute of Management. He taught classes at the Ateneo de Manila University, The Beacon School, Assumption College, and Xavier School. He is the owner of Nautilus Graphic and Visual Designs, a small graphic design studio, and is the publisher of Chamber Shell Publishing which published the National Book Award winning *Siglo: Freedom, Siglo: Passion*, and *The Mythology Class* by Arnold Arre. He is the co-creator of the comic series *Cast* and the National Book Award nominated all-ages detective comic series *Private Iris*.

Carlomar Arcangel Daoana is the author of four collections of poetry, with *Loose Tongue: Poems 2001-2013*, published by the University of Santo Tomas Publishing House in 2014, as the most recent. His other collections, *The Fashionista's Book of Enlightenment* and *Marginal Bliss,* were finalists to the Manila Critics Circle's National Book Awards. In 2012, Daoana received First Place honors in the Carlos Palanca Memorial Awards for Literature in the English Poetry category for his collection, *The Elegant Ghost*. Internationally, his poems have been anthologised in the *Vagabond Asia Pacific Poetry Series* (Sydney and Tokyo) and *Naratif Kisah* (Kuala Lumpur). He was also selected as an international panelist for the 1st Kuala Lumpur Literary Festival held in 2016. A regular arts and culture columnist for the broadsheet, *The Philippine Star*, Daoana teaches poetry writing, art writing, and other fine arts courses and is currently the chairperson of the Fine Arts Department of the Ateneo de Manila University.

Glenn Diaz's second novel *Yñiga,* on the spate of political killings in 2000s Philippines, was shortlisted for the 2020 Novel Prize. Born and raised in Manila, he's currently pursuing doctoral studies at the University of Adelaide in South Australia.

Christine Veloso Lao is an Assistant Professor of the Department of English and Comparative Literature, College of Arts and Letters, University of the Philippines Diliman. She is currently working on a Ph.D. in creative writing at the same University. Her collection, Musical Chairs: Stories, was a finalist of the 19th Madrigal-Gonzalez Best First Book Award. She attended the University of the Philippines National Writers' Workshop as a fellow for poetry, and the Silliman National Writers' Workshop as a fellow for fiction. Her poems have appeared in *Likhaan* and *Kritika Kultura*, and her stories, in the anthologies *Sigwa: Climate Change Fiction from the Philippines; Maximum Volume: Best New Philippine Fiction 2014; Lauriat: A Filipino-Chinese Speculative Fiction Anthology*, and in three volumes of *Philippine Speculative Fiction.*

The Illustrators

Andoyman is the illustrator for "September 28". Graphic artist ang kasalukuyang trabaho. Pagkokomiks ang gustong gawin sa buhay. Madalas, procrastinator buong araw. Gamer mula gabi hanggang madaling-araw.

Ara Villena is an illustrator and art director, specializing in children's book illustrations, comics and concept art for animation. She has illustrated over 20 children's books for various publishers, NGOs and government institutions.   She also creates illustrations for motion graphic videos and animated films. She was awarded the Grand Prize Winner by the 2018 PBBY-Alcala Prize for her illustrations for Becky Bravo's story, *May Alaga Kong Bakulaw*, which was published by Adarna House in 2019. She also won Best Komiks, Best Writer and Best Illustrator awards in the 2020 Komiket Awards for her independently published comic book, *Laya*.

Arnold Arre is a comic book artist, writer and self-taught animator from the Philippines. He has won National Book Awards for his graphic novels *The Mythology Class*, the first to win in the comic book category, and *Trip to Tagaytay*. Aside from comics, he has worked on numerous illustration and design jobs, from music packaging for rock bands to animated music videos for the National Historical Commission. *Milkyboy*, his first animated short film completed in 2013 won 1st Prize at the 25th Gawad CCP Alternative Film and Video Awards (Animation), Best Screenplay at the 7th Animahenasyon, and the Linda Mabalot New Directors/New Visions Award at the 30th Los Angeles Asian Pacific Film Festival (LAAPFF).

MA Bungay is a student, artist, and designer. She is currently a senior at the Ateneo de Manila University, taking Information Design and minoring in Development Management. As an artist, she mainly focuses on digital techniques but also dabbles in oil and acrylics. She is particularly fond of architectural subjects and portraits. As a designer, she specializes in brand identity, campaigns, web, and editorial design. She dabbles in typeface design and digital illustration. She believes that art and design, above all, must be human-centered and rooted in creating more inclusive spaces for people to be brought together to share stories and experiences that make us feel less alone. You may visit her online art journal at mabungayart.tumblr.com and her designer portfolio at abiebungay.design.

Danicole Cuevas is an illustrator and graphic designer whose works consist of conceptual illustrations, portraits (traditional and digital), and printed materials. She loves participating in projects related to children, the environment, and Philippine culture. She believes that art plays an important role in our daily lives in attaining order and comprehending life's complexities.

Crisostomo D., the artist of "Baptism by Fire", is an aspiring artist and graphic designer. This is their first published illustration.

Patricia "PATMAI" G. de Vera is a freelance illustrator, animator, motion graphics artist by trade. She became a recipient of the Adobe Community Residency Fund back in 2020 in Illustration and Animation. Aside from being a college instructor, she's done designs, illustrations, editorial work, and artworks for notable clientele, including UNIQLO PH, Bayer, Adobo Magazine, Philippine Star, Intel Philippines, and more. A registered ISBN-illustrator, her recent published illustration work was for *Challenging the Black Dog: A Creative Health Journal* and *Silencing The Inner Ghosts*. She aspires being able to create elaborate fantasy worlds and in creating the childhood of future generations through her visual story-telling. She recently became a part of the official selection for the 2023 Philippine International Comics Festival (PICOF).

Jon Idago is the illustrator for *Angel of Shadows*. For nearly a decade, Jon worked as a professional Graphic Designer, Illustrator and Animator in an international and multicultural communication agency in Brussels, Belgium. He became an investor at the age of 28 and evolved into becoming an entrepreneur a few years later. He is the Managing Director of Charis Enterprise, a certified John C. Maxwell coach and the CEO of Limitless Personal Development. His most profound passion as a professional is to create jobs and do so for the rest of his life. Jon is presently residing in Belgium with his wife, Krystle, daughter Zoe and sons, Mathieu and Noah.

Nicolai Maverick is a professional illustrator and cultural worker. Currently a member of Artista ng Rebolusyong Pangkultura, a collective of artists immersing and organizing fellow artists all over the country to fight for the rights of the peasant sector and for true agrarian reform in the Philippines.

Jewel Tan is a senior student in the Interactive Entertainment and Multimedia Computing course (better known as Game Design and Development) at College of Saint Benilde. She is primarily a digital artist and an aspiring animator, with most of her work focusing on character design and illustrations. She enjoys putting symbolism and discussing concepts in art, open to hearing new ideas and different perspectives on a topic. Her interests involve watching video games, playing games such as Dungeons and Dragons, and reading analysis on shows she likes. She also participated in online charity events such as Draw4Charity for Child's Play.

The anonymous artist who illustrated "Self-Proclaimed Hero" would simply like to be credited as "a man who wishes an end to this devilry."

ACKNOWLEDGMENTS

The editors and publisher would like to thank the following people for all their help in the development of this project:

Karina Bolasco for her guidance and for providing the idea of having mentorship be the core of this project.

Martin Villanueva for his support, for challenging us to go beyond the initial scope of this project, and for signing us up with the Areté Sandbox Residency Program.

The team at Chamber Shell Publishing and Nautilus Graphic and Visual Designs for managing the design, production, and distribution of this book: Danica Cuevas, Jessa delos Santos, Dylan Puri, Pam Garing, and Cynthia Arre; as well as our interns: Bernardine De Belen, Cydney Mangubat, Katrina Davila, Agustin Sy, Carlos Yap, Rocio Castillo, Sergei Lim, Liam Caro, Vince Manese, Gabrielle Domingo, and Maria Larga.

The administrative team of Areté, both in 2018 and 2021, for providing us with a home and giving us assistance in getting the word out about our project, specifically Maitel Ladrido, Arielle Acosta, Vanessa Reventar, Karlo Erfe, Noriel Mendoza, and Senada Gomez.

The Diocese of Kalookan (Caritas Kalookan Inc.) for allowing us to join in their amazing work of helping those affected by EJK, specifically Sister Ma. May Cano, OP and Bishop Pablo "Ambo" Virgilio S. David , DD. Special thanks to Joy Candelario and Freddie Bernardino for connecting us with Fr. Ambo.

Our Areté focus group discussion panelists: Guelan Luarca, Gino Trinidad, Niño Leviste, and John Nery for their valuable feedback and insights.

Lea and Ray Arsenal, and Nina Salupare of Yellow Sun Studio for their great videography and editing of the student writer interviews.

Missy Maramara for giving our team and student authors a greater understanding of both empathy and ourselves with her wonderful improv workshop.

Paolo Herras for helping us find illustrators from the Philippine comic community willing to contribute to this project.

Fr. Nono Alfonso, SJ and Justin Pontino of Radyo Katipunan for helping us promote the book; and Cholo Mallilin for linking us with Fr. Nono.

Our friends in the local theater community, specifically Floy Quintos, Mae Paner, Missy Maramara, Guelan Luarca, Teetin Villanueva, and the cast and crew of "The Kundiman Party", "Desaparesidos", and "Tao Po" for your artistry, caring, and passion that inspired us to use our art for good.

Carlomar Daoana's Ateneo students from FA 102 sections A and B (Second Semester SY 2018-2019) for their wonderful art installations and pieces that were inspired by some of the stories in this publication and exhibited in Areté in 2019.

Mike Jugo, Rhea Bautista, and the rest of our families and friends who provided us with all the love and support during this whole process. Our vision for a more empathetic, caring, and inclusive future is for you all.

Sam, Amiel, Red, Pat, Jan, and Kat, whose sincerity and passion kept us oldies going.

This book would not have been possible without all your help and we are eternally grateful to you all.